M.I.C.E.

and the

STONE

William Coniston

Wm Coniston

ACKNOWLEDGMENTS

My family and the friends who have been kind enough to look at my work have all provided encouragement, inspiration, advice and constructive criticism. I could not have come this far without them and I offer them my sincere thanks. I am particularly grateful to Matilda Downs and Carl Moore for making the cover.

1

A BLACK STONE

A postman limped up the Peterson's path and put a padded envelope through the front door letter box. As Tilly was leaving for school she picked it up and saw it was addressed to herself and her brother Olly. She quickly opened it and something hard fell into her hand. There was a letter wrapped round it.

'Twenty past,' warned her mother loudly from the kitchen.

At the last minute as usual, Tilly yanked the door open and hurried out, putting the something into her bag for later. A neighbour walked past with his two Yorkshire Terrier dogs.

'Did tha see me bite t'postman,' said a voice.

'Nearly died laffin',' said another voice.

Tilly shook her head. She knew it was impossible but, for a moment, she thought the dogs had spoken. Then the bus came round the corner and she had to run.

That evening Tilly and Olly had a good look at the object from the envelope. It was a shiny black stone about the size and shape of an egg but at the small end were two oval fins like stubby wings. The letter was from Grandpa. He and Granny lived at Scar Bay, a small village on the North Yorkshire coast:

Dear Olly and Tilly,

It's time I passed this on to you. My grandfather gave it to me when I was 13 like Olly is now. He said it belonged to an ancestor of ours called Alfred Peterson who lived near here at Scar Point many centuries ago. My grandfather always said it might be a key to something and it was important to keep it safe in case it was needed.

We can talk more about it when I next see you.

Love - Grandpa.

P.S. Please keep this secret – even from your mother and father. They won't understand.

The children wanted to phone Grandpa about it there and then but there was too much risk of being overheard. They decided they had better wait – even though it was very frustrating.

Later Olly saw a bat fly into the garden shed through a broken window. He was surprised because he knew that in early December bats would normally be hibernating.

The next evening, as he was having another look at the stone and re-reading the letter, he thought he heard a voice in the kitchen saying 'Bulldogs!' like a swear word but when he looked there was nobody there except Bobby the cat staring at an empty milk saucer.

The following morning before anyone was awake a large grey bird appeared at Olly's bedroom window. It tapped on the glass with its beak but Olly did not stir. He was fast asleep on his back, arms stretched out sideways. After a while the bird gave an irritated squawk and flew off.

The bird tried again in the evening, this time at Tilly's window just as she was getting into bed. She heard tapping, drew back the curtain and shrieked in astonishment, but something in the way the bird looked at her stopped her running away.

'Olly,' she called in an urgent whisper, 'quick!'

He rushed in from his room next door. Amazed, he stared at the bird and its bright, inquisitive eyes.

'It's a heron,' he said.

For a moment it seemed to look straight at the black stone on Tilly's bedside table. Then it took off into the night. It was not the only creature to see the stone. The bat from the shed, on a routine fly-past, saw it through Tilly's window. His orders were to keep watch and return to the coast before dawn. Long before the eastern sky began to brighten he was hanging upside down in the eaves of the home of his two mistresses, replenishing his energy with a snack of earwigs and beetles. About an hour later a skinny old lady climbed the loft ladder and the bat crept on to her shoulder to whisper in her ear. She listened quietly for a few moments.

'Well done, Wartwing,' she intoned in Bat and fed him a cockroach from her coat pocket.

2

HIJACK

Liam and his friend Ian were in Liam's bedroom working on a mobile phone bugging system when the yellow rescue helicopter thundered past, low enough to make the whole house shake.

It headed out into the bay and the two of them had a clear view once they had squeezed their way to the window past stacks of electronic equipment.

The helicopter was always a dramatic sight, especially when saving someone, but today it was just practising. They watched it hover as one of the crew was winched into the sea to save an inflatable swimmer.

'I'd love to fly it,' said Liam, wistfully taking in every detail through his thick glasses.

'In your dreams,' said Ian. 'It takes years of training. Even if you could reach the controls from the pilot's seat.'

Liam had to admit that he was not big enough but to him it did not matter.

'No, really,' he said earnestly. 'You could easily hot-wire one.'

Ever since he could remember he had loved computers. Not just using them but finding out how they worked and making them. He would rummage through rubbish bins looking for discarded laptops, broken TVs or anything he could take to pieces for the parts. Every evening he'd be up in his room, which was more like a workshop, peering at wiring diagrams and soldering tiny circuit boards. He'd be so absorbed in what he was doing he could easily forget to eat or sleep.

'Just like his Grandad,' his mother would say, half frustrated, half proud. It was rumoured that Liam's Grandad had invented the computer mouse. He and Liam had spent a lot of time together while he was alive.

Liam was always making something electronic but his latest creation and current prized possession was a pocket-sized tablet that was faster and more complex than most advanced full-sized computers.

Ian was interested in all sorts of technology too and although he did not have quite the same skill and flair as Liam, he was not far behind.

The helicopter landed on the beach not far away. It was time for the crew's tea break.

'I dare you,' said Ian, grinning.

Liam's eyes widened for a moment and he scratched his ear thoughtfully.

'Right,' he giggled as he made up his mind. 'Come on.'

Grabbing a tool kit and the tablet he headed for the door.

Ian followed, pleased that Liam had taken up the challenge but also, if he was honest with himself, a little uneasy as to where it might lead.

The pilot and his two colleagues strolled over to sit on the sea wall with tea flasks and a packet of biscuits, a hundred metres or so from the helicopter. They were not supposed to leave it unattended but there was no-one else near on the beach and with the open side door of the helicopter facing towards them they could keep an eye on it. Luckily the low winter sun was behind the helicopter so its dazzle prevented their seeing Liam and Ian's stealthy approach. Using the undercarriage as cover they sneaked quickly inside and headed for the cockpit.

Liam clipped a torch to his glasses, crawled under the main instrument panel and lay on his back with just his feet poking out. Ian heard him making appreciative noises as he studied the wiring.

Prodding around with a screwdriver and other tools he gave Ian a running commentary on what he was doing.

'That should do the trick,' he said after a couple of minutes. 'At least, it will once I find the main bus node…'

'The what?' Ian said as a flash of blue light cracked under Liam's probe, making both of them jump.

'Oops – found it,' said Liam. 'Now for the test,' he added as he wriggled out, pulling trailing wires. He stood up, turned off the torch and smiling, nervously Ian thought, plugged the wires into the tablet along with a small joystick.

Ian started to get cold feet.

'You're not seriously going to fly this thing are you? What about the crew? They'll see what's happening before we get off the ground. We'll be found out.'

'Don't chicken out on me now,' Liam said, half frightened too, as he clambered onto the pilot's seat, then up to sit on its back so he could see through the windscreen.

He tapped the tablet with a flourish

The helicopter's engine whined into life and the crew shouted in surprise. Tea forgotten, they leapt up and started to run towards it. The rotors turned, slowly at first, then much faster and the din became deafening. Clouds of sand blew into the air, blinding the running crew and slowing their progress.

Looking straight forward, Liam gently moved the joystick and the whole machine started to lift.

Ian panicked. 'Alright alright you've proved your point. For heaven's sake let's get out of here.'

'You mean that way?' asked Liam, pointing upwards.

'No!' yelled Ian, dismayed. The crew had almost reached them.

'OK,' said Liam, very excited yet trying to sound casual.

He killed the engine but instead of making a run for it, paused and gazed dreamily at the horizon, his mind a whirl of microprocessors and binary sequences. It felt as though Grandad was with him and enjoying the moment, feeling proud that his grandson was following in his footsteps. It made Liam feel good.

Ian had seen it before and was not impressed. He leapt up to the pilot's seat and snatched the tablet from Liam, pulling wires free from the instrument panel. Liam slid to the floor, still in a trance.

'Come *on*,' said Ian, dragging his dazed friend to hide behind a stretcher near the main door. Not a moment too soon.

The pilot, a tall man with big feet, was the first to bound into the helicopter. As the rotors came lazily to rest he dashed forward to the empty cockpit. Ian saw his chance.

'Go,' he hissed urgently to the still fuddled Liam, giving him a push.

Unnoticed, they jumped out of the door to the ground. Fresh air and being prodded by Ian brought Liam back to normal.

The puzzled crew searched thoroughly but, finding no-one, stood scanning the beach for possible intruders making their escape.

Lost to sight on the pebbly foreshore, the two mice could hardly run for laughing.

3

THE SCAR TOMB

On Thursday Mr and Mrs Peterson announced they were going to re-paint the kitchen at the weekend and it would be much easier if both children were 'out of the way'. They were kind parents but very absorbed in their own affairs and their jobs. Olly was due to be away on a school activity weekend anyway so Tilly needed somewhere to go.

'She must come over here,' said Granny on the phone. Tilly was pleased. She loved Scar Bay and it was near enough to the Peterson's West Yorkshire home to go for a weekend.

On Friday afternoon Tilly's mother picked her up from school and took her to Bingley station to catch a train for Scarborough via Leeds. Tilly carried clothes and other essentials in a rucksack. She had the Stone too because she and Olly had agreed it would be a good opportunity to find out more from Grandpa.

Although Tilly was two years younger than Olly she was used to the journey, having done it several times before. At Scarborough she changed to a bus that meandered northwards up the coast road with bleak North Yorkshire moors on one side and sea on the other. A few miles short of Whitby the bus turned off the main road for a steep descent to Scar Bay, by which time it was dark and she could see the twinkling lights of the village ahead.

The moon was up and beyond the village she could make out the wide sweep of the bay. On the far side, to the south, was a dark headland with high cliffs. She knew this to be Scar Point which Grandpa's letter had mentioned.

He was waiting to meet her at the bus stop, well muffled up against the cold wind. Together they walked, steeply down again, to the cottage that Granny always described as 'two up and two down'. Strictly speaking it was 'three up' because there was a bathroom upstairs as well as two bedrooms. Downstairs there was just a living room and a kitchen.

'Granny's round at Mrs Hutton's,' said Grandpa. 'They're discussing arrangements for the Antiques and Collectors Fair next weekend.'

It had taken less than three hours to get there but Tilly always felt it could hardly be more different from home.

The sound of the sea was always in the background and above it the haunting cry of sea birds – herring gulls, kittiwakes, oystercatchers. The air had a salty, fishy smell. The village had ancient origins and had not changed for generations. Its rows of tiny houses, clinging close together, looked as though they were tumbling down the hill into the sea.

At the bottom of the village was a slipway, known locally as 'the Dock', down which generations of fishermen had hauled their boats, and up which on moonless nights generations of smugglers had hauled kegs of brandy and other illegal goods.

It was said that there used to be secret passages between houses in the village so that smugglers could hide their contraband. There were no smugglers now and, sad to say, few fishermen. The village was mainly a holiday resort.

There was only one proper road through it, a steep one down to the Dock and the beach. Otherwise there were just narrow alleyways between the houses, not wide enough for cars. Tilly and Olly had explored them all years ago.

Tilly quickly ate the sausage and mash that Granny had left for her in the oven and was soon sitting in front of the fire with a cup of tea. Grandpa sat opposite in his favourite armchair. Through the curtains she could hear wind battering at the window and, a little further away, sea crashing onto rocks at the foot of the cliff.

'You got the Stone, I take it?' asked Grandpa quietly.

'Yes but Olly and I are dying to know what it's for.'

He fell silent, staring into the fire, and it struck her how like Olly he looked. Much older but, like Olly and Tilly, with deep blue eyes and dark hair – his greying now of course. She waited patiently for him to speak.

'Look,' he said finally, 'I don't know if there's anything in it or whether anything will happen but it's best to be on the safe side. Peterson grandparents have a duty to pass it on to their grandchildren. That much I did learn from my grandfather and I think it's the right time to tell you what he told me.'

He paused again. Tilly sipped her tea.

'Scar Bay got its name from the family who owned the castle and estate at Scar Point over a thousand years ago. There were two brothers – Edwin Scar, a fine noble young man and Odric his younger brother who was the opposite of Edwin in every way – mean, devious and cruel. Odric was left in charge when Edwin was called by the King of Northumbria to fight in a war with a neighbouring kingdom. The country was divided into seven kingdoms in those days. Edwin took about forty men with him – over half the castle guards – including our ancestor Alfred Peterson who was their Captain. He and Edwin became firm friends.

'While they were away Odric spent lavishly on the best of everything for himself. Merchants from the Far

East often sailed into Whitby with fine foods, spices and silks and he became their best customer. Among other things they introduced him to a white powder to smoke in a pipe. A drug, of course, very addictive and very expensive.

'So he soon spent the family fortune. He put up rents on the Castle estate to such high levels that tenants and their families starved because they had no money left to buy food. But even that wasn't enough. To get yet more money he re-opened an old jet mine – you know what jet is I presume?'

Tilly nodded – she knew it was a shiny black semi-precious stone that could be found locally, sometimes even among pebbles on the beach. Several shops in Whitby sold jet jewellery.

'Well,' said Grandpa, 'he paid thugs to force people from the village to work in the mine – even women and children. He paid no wages and treated them brutally. Many died or were disabled.'

Tilly was horrified.

'Odric's nastiest thug was called Botwulf. Cunning and strong he soon rose to be Odric's right hand man. He also claimed to be a sorcerer having been apprenticed to a circus magician as a youth. In ancient times science and magic were often confused.'

'Odric's addiction made him fanatical about the jet that brought him the money to buy the white powder. He dressed only in black and required his servants to do the same. At the castle, the carpets, drapes and decorations, once colourful and cheery, were changed to black. It became a dark unhappy place. It's said that even Odric's eyes turned black and somehow shone with piercing darkness. The mine became very extensive, its tunnels reaching right under the bay and beyond. Some say they stretched as far as Whitby.

'There were also secret passages from the mine to most of the cottages in the village. In his madness Odric would watch the villagers through spy holes. Sometimes at night he would appear in a cottage through a secret door to kidnap a child for the mine or to punish someone who spoke ill of him.'

Tilly shivered and drew nearer the fire.

'When Edwin and Alfred came back from the war a couple of years later they were angry and appalled at what they found. Together with the troop of brave men who had fought alongside them, they defeated Odric and his gang in a big battle. Odric and Botwulf fled to a stronghold in the deepest part of the mine but were eventually found. Odric is said to have taken poison rather than face capture and his body was sealed up in the cavern where he fell. My grandfather called it the Scar Tomb.'

Tilly needed to remember all the details for Olly but there were some loose ends.

'What became of Botwulf, Grandpa?'

'As far as I know he was never seen or heard of again. Maybe he just sneaked away, glad to escape with his life, or went back to the circus.'

'What about the mine? Is it still there?' If it was, she thought, she would try to find the entrance tomorrow.

Grandpa smiled. 'I thought you might ask that because I did too when I was a boy. I wanted to find the mine and explore it but my grandfather said that Edwin and Alfred had it flooded with seawater to prevent it from being used again. Edwin didn't need money from jet because the King had been generous with gifts of gold and land elsewhere so he never lived at the castle. He had it sealed up and I suppose it's long since fallen down. He returned to the service of the King.'

'So how does the Stone fit in?'

'As I said in the letter, I really don't know. My grandfather said it was made by Odric and Botwulf but heaven knows what for. You and Olly just keep it safe. You never know when it might be useful.'

'By the way,' he added, 'your Granny thinks the whole story's nonsense so don't mention it when she's around.'

Tilly agreed and was just going to tell him about the heron-on-the-windowsill when there was a blast of cold air from outside as Granny bustled in. She hugged Tilly vigorously then started fussing about how late it was and Tilly found herself heading up the tiny staircase to bed. Her bedroom was the one above the kitchen with twin beds, where she and Olly slept when they visited.

Her eyes closed almost as soon as she got into bed and she began to drift off.

Tap tap tap. The King of Northumbria had come into the room through a secret door and was tapping the bowl of a pipe on the heel of his boot. Her eyelids fluttered and opened a crack so that she could see him properly – but of course he was not there. Smiling to herself, she closed her eyes again and at once began sliding down the velvety slope into a deep sleep.

Tap tap tap. It was on the outside of window but she did not hear.

4

IAN

Priority Encrypted Email
To: Chairman, M.I.C.E.
<aristotle.badger@mice/leeds.org.uk>
From: M.I.C.E. Representative, East Coast
 <wickfeather.gannet@mice/sb.org.uk>
Thursday 4 December 2.30 p.m.

Subject: Tunnels at Scar Bay
Today when I dropped in here for a routine visit, our Section Leader came to me with a strange story. His name is Ian, one of my best mice. He has found something disturbing underground, in tunnels we did not know existed.

I asked him to record a voicemail report, in Rabbit of course, which I attach for you to hear. I should add that he has shown exceptional daring for a mouse and should be highly commended.

As ever, I send you my respect and friendship.
Wickfeather.

Attachment: Ian's Story.mp3
For the past few weeks I've been worried about wild mice being injured and one was even killed. They live outside the normal mouse community – in country burrows instead of the more usual cavity walls and secret places of human homes but they're just as entitled to M.I.C.E. protection as any creature so I investigated.

By asking around I found that most of the trouble had occurred in some tunnels that I didn't know about because they aren't used by civilised mice. There were garbled reports of a fierce beast, so I took a look for myself.

The entrance was through a small hole under the phone box at the Dock but once inside the tunnels were large enough even for humans to use. Some colleagues and I kept watch in relays for several days and nights near where the last few attacks were said to have taken place. Early in the morning of the third day, I'd been on duty all night and was due to be relieved. Everything had been quiet and I was just having a cheese sandwich when I heard someone approaching in the darkness. Assuming it was my relief, I called out quietly: 'Is that you, Liam? Like a snack?'

'No thanks,' came the reply in perfect Mouse, 'but I'll get you on the way back.' And a grinning cat pushed its face right up to mine.

'Lucky for you I can't stop right now,' it said, so close I could see all its teeth and smell its bad breath. Then it padded off down the tunnel.

I don't mind telling you, my legs turned to jelly and I had to sit down for a while but I did recognise the cat. It was Meanwhisker who lives with the old Boyle sisters at the sweetshop.

So I was able to tell the wild mice that there was no fierce beast, just Meanwhisker. I advised them to avoid those tunnels if possible but if they had to use them they should be very, very careful and take all the usual anti-cat precautions. You know, scent neutralisers, personal alarms, catpins and so on.

But then I began to ask myself some questions. How did Meanwhisker get into the tunnels? The only entrance we knew about was too small for a cat. Where was she going in such a hurry and why? So I did some more investigating. I stationed some of my section in the walls of the Boyle sisters' shop. They reported strange things.

First there were conversations in Cat between the sisters and Meanwhisker. Very unusual. Then comings and goings of bats in the loft, with the Boyle sisters receiving messages and giving instructions in Bat. Even more unusual.

Like all mice I'm pretty good at understanding human speech and Cat, though not speaking either of course, and fairly fluent in Rabbit because most creatures learn at least a bit, but Bat's so obscure that few can grasp it. This meant we couldn't tell what messages were coming and going, so we rigged up secret microphones to record them for translation by experts.

We also put a spycam in the shop and found out how Meanwhisker gets into the tunnels. There's a flight of steps hidden below a loose slab in the stone floor. I decided to follow on her next trip.

Nothing happened for a few days then yesterday morning the sisters opened the entrance for Meanwhisker and off she went. I allowed a few minutes for her to pass under the telephone box, sprayed myself with scent neutraliser and slipped into the tunnel behind her. She travelled fast and obviously knew where she was going. It was all I could do to keep up. I couldn't use my torch for fear of giving myself away but I had to be sure-footed and silent as I ran. It was scary.

I was amazed how far we went and the extent of the tunnels. We passed turning after turning, junction after junction and I was worried about finding my way out again but gradually I realised that whenever there was a choice of direction, Meanwhisker always took the tunnel leading downwards. It was two hours before she reached her destination so we must have been very deep and a long way up the coast from the village.

Ahead I saw dim light coming from an open doorway

in the tunnel wall. The door was thick wood, blackened with age, and very strong-looking with iron studs and bolts. Meanwhisker went in but I didn't dare follow. Instead I tiptoed past the door and caught a glimpse of a short passage with a similar door at the far end and just before it some steps leading down to the left. I stood against the wall and listened. I heard Meanwhisker speaking, and there was another voice – a cold, croaking whisper that sounded harsh and cruel and sent shivers down my spine.

Then Meanwhisker came trotting out into the tunnel again looking pleased with herself. No doubt she was relishing the thought of catching a few mice on her way home. She stopped and sniffed and I realised my scent neutraliser was wearing off. I pressed myself harder against the wall behind the door. She was looking round suspiciously and would see me any second. I could almost feel her sharp teeth.

But I had a stroke of luck. The cold, croaking whisper called Meanwhisker back into the passage. I didn't need to think – I ran as fast as I could away from the door and again I was lucky. Without realising it I ran further down into the tunnel instead of back towards the village. If I'd gone the other way, Meanwhisker would pretty soon have caught me up.

After a while I had to stop running because my heart was pounding so hard I thought Meanwhisker might hear it. I could see nothing so I shielded the lens of my torch with a paw and gave a quick flash. Dark tunnel up ahead and damp walls on either side. I listened. Silence, then a faint sound behind. Assuming it was Meanwhisker, I ran off again but hadn't gone very far when I crashed into a wall and winded myself. Another quick flash of the torch and I saw the tunnel had come to a dead end.

I panicked. There were now footsteps behind, coming nearer and nearer. I looked round desperately. There was a small crack in the tunnel wall, barely large enough for half a mouse but it would have to do. Quivering with fear I squeezed myself in as far as I could go and curled up my tail.

It was not Meanwhisker but a bent creature walking on two legs and wearing a ragged cloak with a hood. Possibly it was a very old man – I could just see a long bony nose poking out of the hood. In one talon-like hand it carried a lantern that gave off a weak light that barely greyed the darkness. It passed my hiding place and paused at the dead end to touch the wall. A rock door swung open. The creature entered, leaving the door slightly ajar.

My instinct was to run back towards the village but I could picture telling the story to Liam and the rest of the section – if I made it safely home – and they'd all want to know what was beyond that door. So I forced myself to creep through.

There was a huge cavern with a high, faintly luminous roof. At the centre was an oblong lump of black stone – I suppose you'd call it a plinth or pedestal like a statue would have. Lying on it was a body of some kind but not dead because it stirred and groaned, straining at chains that bound it there.

The bent, ragged creature was pouring a brown liquid down the body's throat.

The stench was awful and there was a sense of evil in the cavern so strong that I had to stuff a paw into my mouth to stop my teeth chattering with fright. I just had to get away from it so I ran off back up the tunnel at top speed. I was lucky to get home in one piece.

Meanwhile the recordings from the Boyle sisters' shop have been translated. Each bat report has been the same: 'No sign of the Stone yet.' Until two days ago when it changed: 'Stone sighted.'

5

DOGGLE HOLE

The morning after Tilly's arrival at Scar Bay Granny and Grandpa said they had to go shopping in Whitby and she was free either to go with them or stay in the village. They would be back at lunchtime. She chose to stay so she could visit her friends Daniel and Kiran Akram who she had not seen since the summer holiday. They were good at keeping secrets so Tilly and Olly had agreed that she should tell them about the Stone and the heron. Now Tilly had more to tell – about the Scar Tomb.

Daniel and Kiran lived in Scar Bay with their parents. Mr Akram was head of the local school. Daniel was about the same age as Tilly and Kiran about the same age as Olly.

Outside the sun was shining but Granny insisted she 'wrap up well'. Why was it, Tilly wondered, that grandparents were so obsessed with warm clothing?

As she stepped out of the back door though, she felt the full force of the cold wind and was glad of her coat, scarf and woolly hat. Firmly holding the Stone she pushed her hands into her coat pockets and strode off.

At the end of the alleyway she turned down the steep main street. From there she could see across the bay but more clearly than in the moonlight of the previous evening. The tide was about halfway down the beach and wind was creating powerful waves that crashed, white and foaming, onto the shingle.

At the top of the beach rose cliffs of brown and grey rock, the height increasing and the colour darkening towards the massive headland of Scar Point.

There was a posh hotel on the headland with big terraced gardens extending to the edge of the cliff and surrounded by thick walls that looked like battlements. Perhaps, thought Tilly, they were the remains of the Scar's castle.

Halfway down the main street she came to Colonel Foster's antique shop. She and Olly liked it because it smelled of wood and polish and was full of interesting bits and pieces, many of them very old. They had known the Colonel and his golden Labrador, Jess, for about two years.

Colonel Foster was a tall middle-aged man with square shoulders and a weather-beaten complexion. A sandy coloured moustache covered his top lip and his hair was the same colour, though starting to grow grey at the temples. He had retired from the army about three years ago. As Tilly entered the shop he was up a stepladder with his back to the door, getting a box down from a shelf. Jess, curled up in a corner, opened one eye.

'Hello,' said a voice, presumably from up the ladder. He must have eyes in the back of his head, thought Tilly. Jess got up and padded over. Tilly knelt to stroke her ears with both hands. Colonel Foster came down the stepladder.

'Hello, Tilly' he said, (I wonder why he said it again, she thought) 'Good to see you. Long time. How's things? Here for the weekend? Jolly cold wind. Sunshine, though. Humbug?'

He held out a bag.

'Thank you very much,' she said, taking one and smiling. He always spoke in short bursts – a bit like gunfire she and Olly thought.

She wondered if she should show the Stone to the Colonel since he was an expert on old objects but something told her to keep it to herself for the moment until she knew more about it. Instead she said, 'Do you think Jess would like to come for a walk? I'm off to find Daniel and Kiran and then on to the beach.'

Then on the spur of the moment she added 'We might go looking for the Scar Tomb. Have you ever heard of it?'

The Colonel seemed to hesitate.

'Heard of it. Could be true. Nasty business. Be careful. You never know.'

'Needs a good walk,' he added, pointing to the delighted animal. Jess had heard the word 'walk' and was already on her feet wagging her tail.

As Tilly and Jess left the shop the Colonel looked after them and his expression darkened.

'Blast!' he muttered under his breath. 'What does she know?'

Tilly continued down the hill with Jess trotting along beside. Where the road became a slipway and swept down onto the beach in a mass of tide-washed cobbles, a sea wall rose on either side. At the top of the wall, on the right hand side, perched the Akram's house. It was a fantastic position. All you could see from the windows was beach and sea. There was a balcony at the front and at high tide waves dashed up against the wall below, sending spray high into the air. Standing there was like being on the bows of a ship and when it was really windy you had to hang on to railings to stop being blown away. You could feel the house shudder when big waves struck but the walls were thick and ancient so there was no danger of their giving way.

'Daniel's up in his room,' said Mrs Akram, smiling, when she opened the door to Tilly and Jess. The familiar sound of Daniel's music wafted downstairs. 'Just go on up. He'll be pleased to see you. You've just missed Kiran.'

'Hi,' said Daniel when she found him. 'I'm having a terrible morning. I was supposed to be going to the football with Dad today but the car's broken down. I'm going to miss the biggest away match of the season and all my school friends will see it and I won't and here I am virtually the only person left in the village.'

Exaggerating as usual, thought Tilly, but he really does look miserable.

'Well,' she said, 'I have something important to tell you and something important to show you but not here. Somewhere no one can hear us like the Nab?'

'Oo good.' Daniel perked up.

In a flurry of arms and legs he flung on two odd socks, wellies, coat and woolly hat, after which they both ran downstairs and out of the house.

'Yes,' shouted Daniel over his shoulder in response to his mother's request for him to be back in time for lunch. He was small for his age but extremely energetic and, of course, mad on football.

The two children and Jess raced down the beach and at the water's edge slowed to a brisk walk. They scrunched along the pebbly shore, dodging waves and throwing sticks into the water for Jess to retrieve. There was no one else about. In summer the beach would have been crowded.

About half a mile along the bay a small promontory called The Nab jutted about a hundred metres down the beach towards the sea. Doggle Hole was a small inlet on the other side of it. The Nab was the first point the tide reached as it came in and if you were in Doggle Hole you could be cut off from the village as the water level rose. But Tilly and Daniel knew a way to climb over The Nab to safety. One of their favourite places was a high cliff ledge near its tip.

Soon they had climbed up to sit on it and Jess parked

herself between them, suspiciously eyeing the gulls wheeling overhead.

'Right,' said Daniel, panting from the climb, 'tell me all this important stuff.'

'Well have you ever heard of Odric Scar or his Stone?'

Daniel had not so Tilly produced the Stone dramatically from her pocket. He leaned across to take a closer look and in his enthusiasm nearly elbowed Jess in the eye.

'Oi, look out.' Tilly heard a gruff voice but not where it came from. It was not Daniel. She looked round but could see no one.

'Did you hear that?' she asked Daniel.

'What, Jess growling?'

Realising what he had done, he stroked Jess's head and whispered words of apology into her ear.

'No, that voice.'

'What voice? I didn't hear one. You're hearing things. Just get on with it,' said Daniel impatiently. It must have been someone down on the beach, thought Tilly.

She told him about the padded envelope, the letter, the heron on the windowsill and what her Grandpa had told her the previous evening. Somehow talking about Edwin, Alfred and Odric, while looking across the bay to the very cliffs they would have known, made it all seem more real. While she spoke Daniel held the Stone, occasionally throwing it from hand to hand or up in the air.

They were both so engrossed they did not notice, high above them, a large bird, about a metre and a half from wingtip to wingtip. It had flown towards them from the village and was now circling gracefully overhead.

Daniel was thoughtful when she had finished her story. 'It doesn't explain what this is for though.'

He lobbed the Stone back to her and she only just caught it. As she did so she heard a voice from above saying quietly but clearly, 'You must be careful with that Stone, young lady.' It was squawky and slightly pompous.

'Who said that?' she asked, looking up.

'What?' said Daniel, also looking up. He had heard a squawk. Seeing nothing they looked down again and yelled in alarm. The bird was now at their level and flying straight at them, long beak first.

Jumping to their feet they tried vainly to claw their way up the rock face behind them.

'Hang on,' Tilly shouted and shut her eyes.

'Oi, shove off!' The gruff voice again.

There was a great beating of wings and it seemed to Daniel that the bird back-pedalled in mid-air just in front of them. Then in a flurry of feathers its feet swung forward and clamped on to the ledge.

Silence descended. Tilly opened her eyes to see the bird carefully folding its wings and settling them into place with prods and pokes from its beak. It was a heron and something about its eyes looked familiar.

'Awkward landing place,' said the squawky voice. It came from the heron.

Tilly turned to Daniel, incoherent noises coming from her mouth. He for his part was quickly getting over the shock of the bird's arrival and was anxious not to alarm it in case its wings opened again and flapped them all off the ledge. Jess growled.

'The bird…it spoke,' Tilly finally blurted.

'Which is not as remarkable as you might think,' said the heron, 'and by the way,' it added testily, 'I'm a male heron not just any bird. Call me Heron. And another thing, you can hear me because of the Stone but it's no use gawping at your young friend and telling him you can hear me because he can't. Not unless he's touching it –

and even then only if you're touching it too.'

It was true. Daniel could not hear Heron speaking. All he knew was that it was squawking and croaking.

Still finding it difficult to speak, Tilly lurched towards Daniel, grabbed his wrist and slapped his hand onto the Stone.

Heron cocked his head on one side and looked at Daniel out of one beady eye. 'Testing, testing. Heron calling.'

Was that a grin? How do you tell if a beaky bird is grinning, Tilly managed to wonder.

'I hear you very well, sir.' Daniel thought he had better sound respectful. He was still worried about beating wings.

'WOW!' he shouted as an afterthought.

'Good,' said Heron, in a business-like tone. 'Now, sit down both of you because I have important things say and not much time.' Obediently and still in shock they sat down without a word.

'Oi, what's going on?' asked a gruff, policeman-like voice behind them.

'Jess!' Tilly and Daniel shouted and burst out laughing.

Heron looked annoyed and Jess puzzled.

If they had not been so busy laughing they might have noticed a flash from the direction of the village, as sun glinted off the Colonel's binoculars.

6

HERON'S MESSAGE

'If you've quite finished,' said Heron severely, as the laughter began to die down.

'Sorry,' said Tilly, suppressing a further giggle, 'By the way, haven't I seen you before – on the windowsill at home.'

'Yes, yes, of course,' said Heron briskly. 'I'd been sent to check you had the Stone *and* I tapped on your window last night but you didn't hear.'

'Er, what's the Stone,' asked Jess patiently, just as Tilly was going to ask Heron who had sent him.

'This black one in my hand.' said Tilly. 'It's letting us understand each other, Can you understand birds?'

'Not unless they speak Dog or one of the better known animal languages such as Rabbit. I don't have much to do with birds. Too flighty.'

'Try touching the Stone. It works with Daniel.'

Heron said just touching Tilly would work in the case of a dog so Jess rested a paw on her knee.

'Hrrm, hrrm,' Heron cleared his throat. 'Before I deliver my messages, I wonder if you could just help me straighten my feathers. This wind today is rather tiresome. There's part of my back that I have difficulty reaching with my beak and with feathers out of place I don't look as good as I should.'

Tilly and Daniel exchanged a quick glance and Tilly said, 'Ok.'

Tilly smoothed and stroked soft feathers while Heron arched his back in pleasure like a cat.

'There,' he said. 'That's fine. Looks better, doesn't it?

My wing feathers are such a refined grey, don't you think? So smooth and elegant. When one has been given such advantages, one really has a duty to make the best of them.'

'Lovely,' said Tilly, with a little too much emphasis, and exchanged raised eyebrows with Daniel.

'This duck's getting on my nerves,' said Jess, raising an ear.

'Heron, if you don't mind,' said Heron, glaring.

They sat side by side on the now rather crowded ledge, Tilly in the middle with Daniel and Jess on either side. Heron faced them, perching on the edge.

'How does the Stone work?' Daniel asked.

'No idea,' said Heron airily, 'but I gather it helps you to tune into other creatures' thoughts.'

'Does it work between humans?' asked Tilly.

'How would I know?' said Heron, starting to sound a bit short tempered. 'Now can we please get on? I haven't got all day and its time I had something to eat. If I don't keep up my intake of fish oil I get irritable and my feathers go dull and floppy.'

'Sorry, we're listening.'

'Right then. I am the Official Messenger and Sentry. It is a very honourable position that was held by my father and his father before him, etcetera, back into the mists of time. Today I am on Messenger business rather than Sentry business so listen carefully.'

Tilly opened her mouth to ask who the message came from but Heron gave her a withering glance so she closed it again.

'Have you heard of the Scar Tomb?' he said.

'Yes,' said Tilly and Daniel in unison.

'Er, no,' said Jess.

Heron rolled his eyes.

'We'll tell you later,' Tilly said hastily.

Jess muttered something inaudible.

'Well,' said Heron, ignoring Jess, 'I've been sent to tell you five things. Firstly, something bad will happen soon unless it's prevented. Secondly, your help may be needed. Your brother's, too, and anyone else with enough courage. Thirdly, watch out for enemies everywhere but particularly in the village.'

Heron paused and gazed at the sky. 'Now, let me see, what were the other two things.'

He looked down at his claws and carried on mumbling while counting them off one by one with his beak. 'Something bad to happen. Help may be needed…'

Tilly and Daniel were beside themselves with curiosity.

'Perhaps,' said Tilly to Heron with what she felt to be great self-restraint, 'it was something to do with who sent the messages, or what's going to happen, or how we can help, or what we should do next, or what… '

'Quite, quite,' Heron interrupted with sudden briskness. He had obviously remembered. 'Please don't interrupt. Fourthly, say nothing to anyone you cannot trust and trust no one unless they have proved themselves. Fifthly, and finally, I am to arrange a meeting with the Chairman of M.I.C.E.'

A second's stunned silence, then 'A meeting with who?' Daniel asked.

'Haddock bladders,' said Heron crossly, looking straight at Tilly. 'More interruptions. It's Saturday today. Just tell me when you and Olly could meet him. It's urgent, it's confidential and it'll take an hour. I assume your home would be the best place.'

Tilly thought so too, provided their parents were out of the way. It would be too difficult to explain things to them.

'Tuesday evening would be best,' she said, 'because

Mum goes to yoga and Dad works late. We get home from school about five and they usually come back about half past seven.'

'Shall we say six then.' said Heron. It was a statement rather than a question. He started to unfurl his wings.

'Wait – please,' said Tilly. She felt they needed a lot more information about every one of the messages and there was one important question above all.

'What's M.I.C.E.?'

Heron's wings were fully open now and he was teetering on the edge of the ledge. 'Oh, that'd take too long to tell you.' He took off.

'Well what do the letters stand for then?' Tilly shouted desperately

'Mammals in Co-operation Everywhere,' came the fading reply as Heron soared out over the sea.

'A bit temperamental, that bird.' growled Jess.

They were so staggered by what had happened that they hardly knew what to say but as they climbed down to the beach they agreed to say nothing to anyone except possibly to Grandpa. Daniel and Kiran would come up to see Tilly after lunch so they could talk the whole thing over.

'We must tell poor Jess about the Scar Tomb, too,' she said, putting her hand on the Stone so that Jess could hear.

'About time,' said the dog.

As they approached the village, still some way off, they saw Daniel's mother come out onto the balcony. 'Food's on the table,' they could just hear her shout. Daniel broke into a run shouting, 'See you later.' Then, 'And it's one all with only a minute of injury time left in this World Cup Final between England and Germany. The ball goes out to the wing, it's going out of play, no it isn't – Akram comes from nowhere and takes possession, look at him run down the field, he's tackled but he side-steps – what a manoeuvre – he's dodging and weaving now as he comes across to the centre, it's a charmed run, no-one can stop him, he's in front of the goal, he shoots… and he scores. The crowd goes wild. And there's the final whistle. Akram scores the winning goal for England…'

Tilly smiled, losing the final words of the commentary, as Daniel disappeared up the slipway, arms high above his head in victory.

The Colonel was shutting up shop for lunch as Tilly passed and agreed to Jess staying with her for the afternoon.

7

ENEMIES

Over lunch, with Granny there, Tilly could not say anything to Grandpa about Heron. Afterwards, just as Tilly had finished helping to clear the table, Daniel appeared, out of breath from running up the steep main street. He gasped hello to the grandparents.

'We'll go upstairs out of your way,' Tilly told them.

'Kiran's on her way,' said Daniel as they reached Tilly's room. Sure enough Kiran was knocking at the door within seconds. They heard her enter, greet Mr and Mrs Peterson loudly then bound up the stairs to burst into the bedroom.

'Tilly!' she screamed, filling the doorway and grabbing her in a great bear hug. In contrast to Daniel, Kiran was tall for her age and had grown so quickly in the past year she had lost track of her own size and strength. She was prone to sudden jerks that caused tablecloths to be pulled off tables or ornaments to fall off mantelpieces.

'I was at ballet this morning,' – Tilly's mind struggled to grasp the concept of Kiran doing ballet – 'otherwise I would have gone to Doggle Hole with you and heard all about this Scar business and met Heron. When I got back I could see you both on The Nab from my window. I knew something was going on because I saw the big bird sitting there on the ledge with you and then taking off.'

Tilly wondered if anyone else had seen them on the ledge.

'By the way,' Kiran added, 'I asked Mum if you could come to tea and she said yes.'

Tilly was happy to agree. Mrs Akram was a very good cook.

'Now where's this Stone thingy?' Kiran added.

They examined it and Kiran and Daniel tried it out on Jess but it did not work for them on their own. They could only tune in if they were touching the Stone while Tilly was holding it. Tilly told Kiran and Jess what she knew about the Scar Tomb and they all puzzled over what the meeting on Tuesday could be about.

'Olly and I will phone you as soon as we can afterwards,' said Tilly.

They were desperate to find other animals to try out the Stone on but remembered Heron's messages about not trusting anyone so decided they had better not.

Instead they went up to the high cliff path with Kiran's kite. She had it with her most of the time as it folded to fit in a pocket. It flew perfectly in the fresh wind and as they watched it soar and dive, the yellow rescue helicopter flew by.

'I'd love to fly it.' said Daniel longingly.

'How could you?' asked Kiran scornfully. 'It takes years of training.'

'I've seen it all on TV,' Daniel replied airily.

'I know how you could get to fly *in* it,' Kiran said.

'How?' yelped Daniel, full of enthusiasm.

'Jump off the cliff into the sea,' she said.

On the way to the Akrams for tea, the children called in at the sweetshop near the bottom of the village. It was quite old fashioned and sweets were still sold from big jars on shelves lining the walls. The quaintness of the shop had always been attractive to Tilly but she found the two old ladies who kept it a bit frightening.

Ingrid and Astrid Boyle were sisters. Both were thin and sharp nosed with straight grey hair pinned close to their heads. Ingrid had a squint so it was difficult to know when she was looking at you. Astrid had a wart on the end of her nose with a hair sticking out of it. They always wore coats and hats, as though they had just arrived or were about to leave. Their words seemed friendly on the surface but Tilly had always sensed a threatening undercurrent.

They were behind the counter when the children went in. A black cat, sleeping on a shelf, languidly opened an eye and shut it again.

'Good afternoon, children,' said Astrid and Ingrid Boyle together. They had a funny way of saying 'children'. It came out like 'chidldrennn' and the 'n' sound at the end went on too long. The ends of many of their words went on too long.

'Hello,' the children replied and started looking round to choose their sweets. Tilly chose sherbet lemons, which Ingrid weighed into a paper bag.

'Did you enjoy your walk on the beach this morninnnng?' she asked as she handed Tilly her change.

'Yes, thanks,' Tilly replied, almost without thinking.

'We thought you mighttt,' said Ingrid, smiling a smile with no warmth and nodding her head. Her loose eye seemed to look over Tilly's shoulder. Astrid was also smiling and nodding.

Tilly's heart missed a beat. Had they been watching? Were they friend or enemy?

Almost certainly not friend, she decided in an instant. She could feel Jess bristling.

'Er…yes. I mean… did you?' she stammered, blushing with confusion.

She added something stupid about it being a bit windy for the time of year and hurried out of the shop. The others quickly followed.

'Those two give me the creeps,' growled Jess. They all felt the same.

'They must have been watching us this morning,' said Daniel, 'but I didn't see anyone on the beach.'

'Attic window, probably,' said Kiran, looking up at the confusion of roofs and dormer windows above them.

Just then Tilly turned to look back up the street. The Boyles had come to the door of the shop. Ingrid was looking down the street after them. Further up on the other side, the Colonel was standing at the door of his shop. Astrid, her wart hair bent in the breeze, was looking straight at the Colonel and he was looking straight at her. Tilly could tell that their eyes were meeting but their faces were expressionless.

Tilly nudged the others and they, too, turned to see the stare. The Colonel, seeing that he had been spotted, pretended to straighten some bric-a-brac outside the shop. Astrid and Ingrid smiled their cold smiles at each other and went inside again.

'Well, what did you make of that?' asked Tilly after they had reached the Akram's house and rushed upstairs to Daniel's room. So that Jess could join in the conversation she touched Tilly's knee with her paw again and the rest of them sat in a circle touching the Stone.

'Those Boyle sisters are too creepy to be trusted,' said Daniel.

Everyone agreed.

'Why were they watching us this morning?' Tilly asked. 'Do they know more than we do? I wish Heron was here. He's our only link with this business. And what about the Colonel? Is he in league with them?'

'It seems like it,' said Kiran. 'The look he was exchanging with Astrid Boyle certainly meant something.'

'Oi!' Jess growled. 'Do you want a good biting? My master's very brave and honourable. In the army he commanded hundreds of men. They all respected him and trusted their lives to him. He's spent his life protecting the country from enemies. He can't suddenly become one himself.'

'We all want to agree with you, Jess,' said Tilly, stroking the dog's silky ears. 'We certainly know nothing bad about the Colonel and if a dog like you feels she can trust him it must count for something but how do we explain the way he was staring at Astrid Boyle?'

None of them could answer that question.

***

The creature was very old yet it moved with surprising agility in the darkness. Beneath its tattered cloak, its spindly arms and legs were in the same place as a man's. Its head and scrawny neck were placed centrally between its shoulders. But human resemblance ended there. Its nose was long and hooked, its face drawn and haggard, little more than a skull with grey skin stretched over it. Its backbone was bent almost double. It had no hair and its leg, arm and finger joints were misshapen and twisted. Twisted almost as much as its once brilliant mind.

Some hours earlier, it had received news that had caused it to ascend from below. Up and up it had scuttled, through an endless labyrinth of tunnels and steps. Now at the surface, yet concealed in the cavity of an ancient wall, it stood with one of its bloodshot eyes to a tiny chink, beyond which it could see into a room. On the floor of the room were three children and a dog.

But the creature's eye was not focussed on them. A sigh escaped from its lips.

'At last,' it breathed. 'The Stone.'

8

M.I.C.E.

Tilly did not notice anything unusual during her journey home on Sunday evening but two large birds were following the bus and the train. One was familiar – Heron – his neck folded in flight mode. The other was white with a golden head, its long black-tipped wings designed for extended flights without rest. When Tilly's train got to Leeds, Heron circled overhead and the other bird began a gliding spiral descent.

Tilly changed to the train for Bingley where her mother was meeting her and Heron followed them home. He stood motionless in a corner of the garden, almost invisible. He had been given strict instructions to keep watch for enemies. The instructions had come from the gannet who had accompanied him as far as Leeds. Wickfeather Gannet was one of the oldest and wisest birds in the country.

Gannets prefer not to let it be known how long they live but they have allowed humans to have enough information to guess their lifespan at about thirty-five years. In fact, it is far longer. Wickfeather was forty-one and could expect to live another thirty years. He was held in great respect by the bird and animal community so had been an obvious choice when the highly secret M.I.C.E. needed to appoint an East Coast Representative fifteen years before. There were only eight Representatives covering the whole United Kingdom and for the four coastal areas – East, West, South and Scotland – gannets had always been selected. They could keep watch further out to sea than any other bird and thought nothing of flying right across the country in a few hours if duty called. They could also think quickly on the wing and were good at organising.

Communication between species in the animal kingdom is less of a problem now Rabbit has become the main universal language, though recently Gopher from the USA – a variant of Rabbit – has been gaining ground. Gannets are excellent linguists and Wickfeather could speak Rabbit, Badger, Gopher, Wildebeest (common in Africa), Reptile Pidgin (reptiles do not speak much) and several others.

When he left Heron, Wickfeather headed to M.I.C.E. headquarters in Central Leeds. Near the Town Hall, which is guarded by four large stone lions, there is a large white building called City Hall. It is easily spotted from the air because of its colour and because it has two towers, each surmounted by a golden statue of an owl. In front of City Hall is Millennium Square and at one corner a small garden with fountains. Deep beneath is the Headquarters of M.I.C.E. The main entrance is in a retaining wall behind a wooden seat.

In the darkness, Wickfeather glided silently down to the gardens, cold and bare at this time of year and deserted apart from a solitary bat hanging in a leafless tree. Wickfeather walked under the seat and poked his beak into a small hole in the stonework. The latest beak and paw recognition software of the electronic lock allowed him in and he went straight to the Council Chamber with its thickly carpeted floor, oak panelled walls and stone vaulted ceiling. He perched in his usual place at the oval table of polished oak.

At the head of the table sat a Badger and there were eight other creatures around it. They represented all species in the various regions of the country and had been elected for their bravery, discretion and good sense.

There were the four gannets (including Wickfeather), two rabbits (representing Rural Areas North and South), a fox (Greater London) and a large Alsatian dog (Urban Areas Outside London).

Normally the Council met once a month to review current threats and make any necessary decisions but this was not a normal meeting.

The general chatter lapsed into respectful silence when the Badger, whose name was Aristotle, stood up to speak. He was old with greying whiskers, not as agile as he used to be, but his eyes were bright and clear, a sign of his intelligence and wisdom.

'Colleagues,' he began, taking off his oval reading glasses and speaking in Rabbit, 'I must apologise for calling you here at such short notice and I thank you for getting here so quickly. The reason for the summons is that Representative Wickfeather has discovered matters of such gravity that it was essential to call this emergency meeting of the Council.

'On Thursday he sent me a report he had received from the Section Leader, Scar Bay. Such a remarkable report that I could hardly believe it. After considering the implications, I made further enquiries from certain sources which I must at this stage keep confidential. Also I set our librarians to study the Books of Abominations and other relevant records. They had to search back further than they had ever done before. It goes without saying that we are speaking of an era long before computer records. We are speaking of parchments so old that they need special preservative treatment before they can be handled, otherwise they turn to dust. We are, in fact, speaking of a time about thirteen centuries ago.'

There were gasps of surprise as he paused and absently stirred his pile of papers on the table.

'I regret to say,' he went on, 'that, as a result of my

enquiries and researches, I am convinced of the complete truth of the report Wickfeather received. Further, the report is proof that one of the most ancient warnings recorded in our Books of Abominations has become fact. It means the probable revival of a wickedness so old that we and generations of our predecessors had forgotten about it. A threat to the entire United Kingdom and possibly beyond. At best the freedom and at worst the lives of countless creatures (including humans) are at risk.

A murmur of alarm went round the room.

'Events are moving quickly and we have no time to lose if we are to prevent disaster,' he went on. 'I have therefore taken certain action for which I will seek your approval later in the meeting but first I will ask Wickfeather to give you his report.'

As he sat down there was an anxious buzz of conversation.

Wickfeather did not need to stand up. He was perching on the back of a chair, like the other gannets.

'Thank you, old friend,' he said to Aristotle, in Badger as a mark of respect, and as the Council quietened down he reverted to Rabbit.

After what Wickfeather had to tell the Council and what Aristotle revealed about his research, there was a shocked reaction and a long debate. The meeting lasted late into the night, studied many ancient texts and only broke up when the members had accepted what Aristotle had done so far and worked out a plan for future action. However, as the members left they were uneasy. They knew they had little choice, yet placing such responsibility on the shoulders of two human children was taking an unprecedented risk.

***

Back home on Sunday night, Olly sat at the bottom of

Tilly's bed and listened in amazement as she told him about Heron, Alfred, Edwin, Odric and everything that had happened.

When she had finished he examined the Stone with a magnifying glass. 'It obviously works,' he said, 'but how? It feels solid and doesn't rattle and there are no joints or screws, so it doesn't look as though there are circuits or moving parts inside it but at least it explains what I heard in the kitchen the other night.' Tilly giggled as he told her about the cat swearing at the empty milk saucer.

'I've got to try this out,' said Olly.

He went downstairs into the kitchen. No-one was there and everything was still disorganised as a result of the parents' painting activities. The contents of cupboards were piled on the table and the floor. The fridge was pulled away from the wall and even the central heating radiator was disconnected and leaning against a chair.

Bobby came in through the catflap and looked around.

'Still no warm radiator and I bet the milk tastes funny again.' Olly heard him grumble.

Mr and Mrs Peterson had not noticed all the dust in Bobby's saucer.

Olly smiled, and without saying anything picked up the saucer, washed it at the sink and filled it with creamy milk from the fridge. Meanwhile Bobby rubbed himself round Olly's ankles.

'Well,' said Bobby sulkily 'at least one member of this household is civilised.'

When Olly put the saucer down Bobby immediately started lapping and purring with pleasure. Olly waited until he had finished and was washing his whiskers.

'Did you enjoy that, Bobby?' he asked quietly. The effect on the cat was electric.

'Yikes,' he shouted, running under a chair, 'who said that?'

'Me,' said Olly, grinning. He held out the Stone. 'I'm using this.'

'What is it?' asked Bobby, sounding shaken, frightened and suspicious all at the same time.

'Don't be scared,' said Olly, reaching under the chair. 'Here, let me pick you up.' And Bobby, who trusted Olly, allowed himself to be picked up.

'You may stroke me if you wish,' he said purring graciously. Olly, smiling to himself, did just that and together they went upstairs to Tilly's room.

'I've just been talking to Bobby,' said Olly as he put Bobby down on the bed. The cat promptly snuggled down, purring again.

The two children touched the Stone.

'I was frightened,' Bobby said, sounding petted. 'Why do I understand you when up to now you've talked gibberish except when you say my name.'

So they told him about the Stone and started tell him about Edwin and Alfred but the cat was far too comfortable and full of creamy milk to concentrate. He yawned, and stretched. This painting going on in the kitchen had been very trying. He closed his eyes and went to sleep, so the children abandoned further explanation.

Olly was excited about using the Stone.

I'll try it on those dogs up the street tomorrow, he thought
That'll surprise them, thought Tilly.

They looked at each other, stunned. Neither had spoken.

They could read each other's thoughts.

This didn't happen with Daniel and Kiran, thought Tilly.
Well it's happening with us.

They also realised that the exchange had taken place

in an instant, much quicker than it could have done with speech. By experimenting they found that it worked when they both touched the Stone and if only one of them was touching it the other could hear thoughts but not send them. It worked between their bedrooms, which were next door to each other, but not over any greater distance.

They were dying to tell someone about it but knew they must not, except that they could confide in Kiran and Daniel when they reported on Tuesday's meeting. But that was two whole days away. How could they wait?

***

Heron kept watch in their garden again on Monday night. He visited the River Aire during the day to get food to keep his fish oil levels up. Mr Peterson would have been surprised to find a pile of trout concealed under some leaves behind the shed. Heron saw Wartwing flitting around at dusk and reported it to Wickfeather the next day. Wartwing spent most of the night in the shed, dreaming of his mistress's cockroach pocket.

***

It is not easy for a badger to move around during daylight so Aristotle generally travelled at night. Monday midnight found him already on his way to the meeting with Olly and Tilly.

The Petersons lived in a semi-rural suburb of Bradford, some distance up the Aire Valley from Leeds. He would arrive before dawn at his cousin's sett on Oaklands Hill, near to the Peterson's house and after his favourite supper of kippers, poached egg, brown bread and dandelion tea he would probably sleep until the early afternoon. By that time the texts and emails that relentlessly pursued him wherever he went and were inseparable from his position as Chairman, would have built up into quite a backlog. Dealing with them would occupy him until he walked to the Peterson's house, passing discreetly through fields and gardens to avoid roads.

Although the first leg of his journey was the longest, it was the least energetic. He was grateful for that, he reflected, as he stepped onto a small boat in an obscure corner of the Leeds canal basin. The boat was a streamlined cabin cruiser made of dark wood, polished to a high gloss. The nameplate on its bows read *S.S. Dauntless*. It had large windows, brass fittings and four comfortable leather seats inside. The wheelhouse was to the rear with a good view over the cabin roof, and a narrow funnel rose above it. Aristotle was the only passenger that evening.

The boat would take him 15 of the 17 miles to his cousin's place, along the Leeds – Liverpool canal but the last two miles would be on foot – uphill, carrying a rucksack and making sure he kept out of sight. It would be quite strenuous but it was good for his health. The demands of his work meant that he did not exercise as much as was advisable for a badger of his age.

'Sh-shall I let off, sir?' said the brown water vole in charge of the boat, quivering a little with nerves and speaking in poor Rabbit. (Voles are not good linguists.) He had appeared at the entrance to the main cabin and held his tiny, almost human, hands together in front of him, occasionally rubbing them over each other as though he was washing them. He had not carried the illustrious Aristotle Bandger on his craft before and it made him anxious.

'Th-that is, I mean,' he went on, the tip of his nose blushing slightly as he realised he had not said it right, 'is it alright if I p-push off, sir?'

His nose turned rose pink as he searched for the right words in Rabbit.

'I mean, s-sir, shall we set off?'

'Fine,' said Aristotle, trying to sound reassuring so as to put the vole at ease. 'Whenever you're ready, Captain. How do you do, by the way, my name is Aristotle. What's yours? Haven't we met somewhere?'

'M-my name is Dauntless Arvicola, sir and I don't th-think we've met but may I say what an honour it is, sir, to have you on my s-steamboat and to be able to help M.I.C.E. in however small a w-way, sir.' His nose blushed an even deeper pink. 'N-not that I mean it is a small thing to have you on my steamboat, s-sir. Quite the c-contrary. I just mean I'm not v-very important, sir, and you are and I am pleased to help M.I.C.E. in however s-small a way. Oh d-dear, here we go again.' He lapsed into distressed silence.

'Listen to me, Dauntless Arvicola,' said Aristotle, amused yet sympathetic, 'I appreciate your help, because I know nothing about steamboats and you do. That's how M.I.C.E. works – everyone contributing their expertise. As to importance, well, I thought you looked familiar and now I remember that I knew your father and your grandfather, who were very brave creatures. I could tell you some amazing stories of their bold deeds on behalf of M.I.C.E. The Arvicolas have a lot to be proud of.'

At that, Dauntless Arvicola's nose turned deep crimson but Aristotle could tell that he was pleased. His shoulders straightened a little, his chest filled out a little and he stopped dry-washing his hands.

'Oh, s-sir, you're very kind. Thank you for remembering my father and grandfather, sir, and I'll try to do j-justice to their memory but really, sir, I d-don't think I could be as b-brave as them, sir, and all I know about is my s-steamboat, sir.' With that he cast off and went sternwards to take the controls.

The engine's precision moving parts had been machined and adjusted to perfection by Dauntless Arvicola and his late father and grandfather, so that when he pulled the lever there was hardly a sound as steel and steam combined in lubricated harmony to turn the propellers.

With the experienced hands of Captain Arvicola at the wheel, the steamboat quietly nosed out into the main canal and headed west.

9

MEETING

The children arrived home from school on Tuesday to find the usual note from their mother telling them how to get their tea ready. They had just finished and the kitchen clock showed five past six when there was a knock at the back door. Tilly rushed to answer it.

Somewhere in the back of her mind she had built up a picture of the Chairman as an elderly gentleman with a waistcoat and grey hair, possibly with a smartly dressed assistant carrying a briefcase. What she actually saw was a large badger wearing a rucksack and, beside him, a big white bird. She let out a yelp of surprise. Olly came up behind her, holding the Stone.

'How do you,' said the badger. 'I trust you are expecting us? May we come in and introduce ourselves. We feel a little conspicuous out here.'

'Of course,' said Olly. Tilly was still open-mouthed and paralysed.

'Get a grip,' Olly hissed.

'Sorry,' she whispered, standing aside to let the two visitors in. 'What did he say?'

'He asked if they could come in.' he whispered. 'Look, you'd better keep touching the Stone.' She put her hand on it at once, regaining her composure a little.

'We're very pleased to meet you at last,' Olly added, louder.

'And we to meet you.' The badger looked round the kitchen. 'The table will do nicely.' Then he peered at the two children closely for moment.

'They are clearly a son and daughter of Alfred.' He

said to the bird, 'Look at the eyes and the hair particularly.'

'Er, actually our father isn't called Alfred,' said Olly.

'Forgive me,' said the badger. 'I did not mean to be rude. All will be explained but first things first. Introductions. My name is Aristotle Badger. I am the Chairman of Mammals in Co-operation Everywhere, which we will tell you about in a minute. May I also introduce Wickfeather Gannet, a long-standing member of the Council and the Representative for the East Coast.'

'I *thought* you were a gannet,' said Olly, 'but I've only seen one through binoculars before so I wasn't sure.'

Wickfeather smiled, at least Olly thought he was smiling. His eyes certainly danced.

'We try not to have too much contact with humans. We prefer to keep to ourselves.'

Aristotle Badger took off his rucksack and positioned himself at one end of the oblong table, while Wickfeather Gannet perched on a chair-back at the other. Olly and Tilly sat beside each other along one side so they could both comfortably touch the Stone.

'Now,' said Aristotle, 'I'd like to start by telling you about M.I.C.E.'

At last, the children thought to each other.

'It's a secret organisation,' he continued, 'set up originally by a small group of higher non-human creatures to counteract the slaughter and misery that humans cause to animals and birds, especially through wars and conflicts of that sort. It had its beginnings in the dark ages more than thirteen centuries ago when the country was torn by violence and lawlessness.

'Some species, particularly mice, are good at understanding human speech so they became spies. They eavesdropped in castles and manor houses across all the seven kingdoms and beyond, gathering information that was studied centrally and used to help non-humans avoid danger. There was also direct action by secret agents. Very occasionally they were human.'

'You mean – people?' asked Olly, surprised.

'Yes but carefully selected. Sometimes influential people in high places. It is, of course, largely because of behind-the-scenes efforts by M.I.C.E., that the seven kingdoms gradually merged to become one.'

He glanced at the clock. 'In a moment Wickfeather will tell you a strange story but I need to mention M.I.C.E. records first.

'Nowadays, of course, they're all digital and M.I.C.E. has a powerful network that connects our branches all over the world but at the beginning the records were parchment books in which were written the threats that arose and action taken to counter them. They came to be called the Books of Abominations.'

'The very earliest Book of Abominations is the one we call The First Book.' He took a thick bundle of papers from his rucksack. 'See, here is a photocopy of one of the first entries. It's about Odric Scar.'

The children looked but all they could see was a mass of ancient writing in a language they did not understand.

'Which brings us to Ian,' said Aristotle.

Ian who? the children thought but before they could ask Wickfeather began to speak.

Olly and Tilly listened spellbound to his account of Ian's adventure in the tunnels.

'Those translated bat messages,' said Tilly when he had finished. 'Where d'you think the bat saw the Stone?' She feared she already knew the answer.

'Almost certainly here,' said Wickfeather. 'Heron has reported bat activity round the house.'

Heron must be here somewhere, they thought.

'I saw a bat last week,' said Olly.

Tilly shuddered. She did not like the idea of being close to bats. Olly was interested in them and would be quite happy to handle one but his mind was already on something else.

'In a way I'm not surprised to hear about the tunnels, because Grandpa has always spoken of legends about them.'

Tilly agreed. When she was much smaller Grandpa had made up exciting bed-time stories about secret passages and magic, with children, usually orphans, performing heroic deeds and finding long lost brothers and so on.

'In fact,' Olly continued, 'what Ian found sounds very like the mines that Grandpa said were flooded. So maybe they weren't flooded after all.'

'We think they weren't,' said Aristotle. 'I'll come to that, though. There's more about the Stone first. Odric tried to make the drug he was addicted to and in the process experimented on mice, rats, rabbits, dogs, birds and any other creatures he could get hold of. He caused untold suffering and many died in terrible agony.

'At the same time Botwulf worked on a way of communicating with the victims so as to make it easier to understand the effects of the drugs administered to them. That is how and why the Stone came into being. Odric and Botwulf tried out prototypes on poor captive creatures, often with appalling results – animals sent mad, having horrible hallucinations or simply dropping dead through brain damage.'

Olly and Tilly were sickened. They knew Odric and Botwulf had been bad but this was worse than they had imagined.

Aristotle read it in their faces.

'Yes,' he said peering at the photocopy he held, 'The

First Book says that the Stone was 'fashioned for evil' but also that it was 'turned to good'.'

'How?' asked Tilly. They would feel better about touching it if it had been used to put right some of the wrongs.

'I'll come to that but I'm afraid it gets worse before it gets better,' said Aristotle grimly. 'Did you hear from your grandfather that when Edwin and Alfred came back from the war, they pursued Odric and Botwulf into the jet mine?' The children nodded.

'Well, down behind a very solid door – the first door that Ian came to – they had a place where they carried out evil animal experiments. Edwin and Alfred were unable to break down the door and explosives had not yet been invented, though there were rumours that Botwulf made them. There were also rumours that he had made many improvements to the Stone so that it not only enabled communication with animals but could also harm them at Odric's will.

'M.I.C.E. sent a small band of fit, highly trained mole soldiers – commandos they would be called nowadays – to steal the Stone from Odric and Botwulf. Moles are fierce underground fighters who can dig tunnels as fast as others can run along them, yet are small enough to keep out of sight. Their mission was successful. They secured the Stone and were able to unlock the heavy door from the inside. Edwin, Alfred and their men rushed in and released the captive animals but Odric and Botwulf fled to a deeper level where they had created an even stronger hiding place – solid rock with a solid rock door so the moles could not penetrate – and there they stayed. Guards were posted outside so they were unable to escape.

'Grandpa said Odric took poison and Botwulf disappeared,' the children said, almost in unison.

'It appears,' Aristotle replied. 'that Edwin and Alfred ordered the existence of Odric and Botwulf to be kept secret and for the story to be put about that Odric killed himself and Botwulf ran away, never to be heard of again.

'The First Book also says that on Odric's orders Botwulf had made the Stone in such a way that Edwin could never use it. Odric and his brother were complete opposites and no doubt Odric was afraid of what might happen to him if Edwin used the Stone. So Edwin gave the Stone to Alfred for safe keeping and Alfred was able to use it to heal creatures that the two villains had injured. Most mammals and birds regard him as one of the great heroes of all time.'

That made the children feel proud.

'So what actually happened to Odric and Botwulf then?' Olly asked.

'The First Book does not say but is quite clear on one thing: Odric and Botwulf will return thirteen centuries after their imprisonment began.'

'When's that?' asked Tilly quickly.

Aristotle spoke quietly.

'Four days from now.'

10

COMMITMENT

There was a thoughtful silence while the children absorbed this bombshell.

How can they return after thirteen centuries and what's this got to do with us?

'So are you saying,' asked Olly out loud, 'that probably Ian saw Odric and Botwulf in the tunnels last week? Because if so I don't see how it's possible. How could anyone survive so long and even if they have why would they wake up at this particular time?'

'There are many questions we can't answer,' Aristotle replied.

'But if Odric does wake up, what then?' said Tilly. 'He's shut in down there and if he and Botwulf try to come out and do something bad the police or the army could capture them.'

'It may not be as simple as that. The First Book tells us that the Stone is the key to waking Odric and if it is allowed to happen he will become so powerful that no army could stop him seizing control of the whole country.'

'Alright then – we keep the Stone and smash it to bits with a big hammer,' said Olly after a moment.' That way he won't wake up even if he could.'

'Apparently Alfred and Edwin tried to smash it, but the strongest men and hammers were unable to make any impression it. And as to keeping it from Odric and Botwulf – that would be a good thing but I suspect Botwulf will come after it.'

'Bury it in a secret place or lock it away in a bank

vault or something then?' said Olly, thinking he'd still like to try a hammer on it.

'That might work,' said Aristotle, 'But tell me, am I right in thinking that the two of you can share each other's thoughts when you touch the Stone?'

The sudden question surprised them but there was no point in denying it.

'Yes, we can,' said Tilly for both of them, 'we found out on Sunday.'

'Just as I hoped,' said Aristotle.

'How did you know?'

'I did not but the First Book leads us to expect this in descendants of Alfred. It may prove to be of great importance.'

Importance for what?

'Alfred studied the Stone,' Aristotle continued, 'and experimented with it but, unlike Odric, he used it for good. To heal, to teach, to resolve conflict and so on. He tried to find a way to prevent its being used for evil but unfortunately did not succeed.

'However, The First Book says he did find a way to restrict use of the Stone to descendants of those who had used it in the past. Odric had no children so that means the Peterson family.'

I wonder where all this is leading, the children thought to each other, not knowing whether to be scared or pleased. They mentally listed living Peterson descendants. There were only four as far as they knew. They could rule out Grandpa because he was too old. They could rule out their father because he was too busy to think about it. So who did that leave?

Us.

Tap, tap, tap. Heron had been keeping a lookout and was now at the window.

'Yoga's just finished,' he said when Olly opened it.

54

That meant Mrs Peterson would be back in ten minutes.

'Right,' said Aristotle, 'I think we've covered everything except, of course, the most important matter of all. Are you willing to help?'

'But how?' Tilly asked. 'By going to a bank with the Stone and putting it in their safe?'

'No,' Aristotle replied. 'As well as saying that the Stone is a key to waking Odric, the First Book also says it can be used to defeat him, so M.I.C.E. – and I agree – thinks that the wisest course is for you to keep the Stone for the time being if you are willing. They do not ask this lightly as they know it could be dangerous.'

'But we have no idea what to do with it or what might happen,' said Olly.

'Nor does anyone,' replied Aristotle gravely, 'but I am confident the way will become clear. At best the time for Odric to wake up will pass with nothing happening. At worst he will somehow wake up and need to be confronted by someone who can use the Stone.'

Us again.

'So what do you say?' he added.

The children flashed thoughts at each other. They were full of questions and fears but mixed with pride that they were the only ones who could use the Stone if help was needed.

Olly answered, Tilly silently agreeing. 'We'll keep the Stone as you ask and see what happens.'

'Very good.' said Aristotle as he and Wickfeather got up to go. 'M.I.C.E. will be very pleased and relieved when I report to them, as am I. We will support you however we can but there is one very important thing. Can you be in Scar Bay this weekend with the Stone? If there are developments that is where they will be.'

The children conferred for an instant. They felt sure Granny and Grandpa would not mind so they said yes.

'Splendid,' said Aristotle, beaming. 'Goodbye for now, then'.

He stepped outside, rucksack on his back, and in a few seconds was lost in the darkness

Before Wickfeather flew silently up into the night sky he too said goodbye, dipping his beak twice, which is the gannet way of showing respect.

***

Later, Aristotle Badger boarded *S.S. Dauntless* at Bingley locks for the journey to Leeds. About half way there, he left his seat and clambered up to the wheelhouse.

'Tell me Captain, have you ever taken your ship up the east coast?'

Dauntless Arvicola twitched and quivered, his nose turning pink.

'N-no, sir' he replied, 'but I once sailed there with my f-father on the *S.S. Dauntless* when I was v-very young. I remember being alarmed, sir, by the s-size of the s-sea. W-why do you ask?'

'I would like you to take me to Scar Bay by early Saturday morning,' said Aristotle.

'M-my goodness,' exclaimed Dauntless Arvicola before he could stop himself. His nose turned deep red. 'The s-sea!'

A mixture of horror and excitement crossed his face.

'Yes,' said Aristotle, 'M.I.C.E. is expecting something to happen there and you would be doing me a great service.'

'Oh, s-sir, it would be an honour,' came the immediate reply but Aristotle could tell from the hesitant silence which followed that if Dauntless Arvicola's hands had not been on the wheel there would have been a good deal of fearful dry hand washing. There was certainly a good deal of twitching and reddening. Finally,

Dauntless Arvicola plucked up courage to speak.

'S-sir, I hope you don't mind my asking but will there be d-danger, sir?'

His nose alternated between pink and deep red.

'I cannot deny that there could be danger but you may be sure, my young friend, that all of us who face it will help each other. If we succeed in our endeavours, we shall prevent a great evil.'

Dauntless Arvicola thought of his wife Prudence and their four babies. How proud they would be at his being asked to help with such mighty events.

'Oh, sir,' he said, 'I will do my very b-best.'

Aristotle's reply was brisk. 'Good, I can ask no more. Now when must we leave and what will be our route?'

Thanks to Dauntless Arvicola's father and grandfather there was a comprehensive collection of charts aboard.

***

The same evening Colonel Foster lifted a shabby briefcase down from his loft and took out a tattered leather volume. Its ancient contents were handwritten, not all by the same person. Every word of the text was already familiar to the Colonel but he needed to check it over one last time.

'Time's definitely come,' he muttered to himself when he had finished reading.

Jess, snoozing at his feet, stirred uneasily. She picked up a lot from her master's tone of voice. He was anxious.

11

PLANS

Just before going to bed, Olly and Tilly shared their thoughts on the whole situation, using the Stone. It was faster than talking and there was no chance of parents overhearing.

They had been given lots of information but none of it even hinted at what they would have to do. Aristotle had mentioned it could be dangerous, but all they really knew was that they must go to Scar Bay at the weekend and be ready for anything.

That was the first thing to arrange.

Mum and Dad are still working on the kitchen, sent Olly *so they wouldn't mind us being away. I'll ring Grandpa tomorrow evening. What are we going to do with the Stone, though. If it's needed for Odric to wake up I still think it might be better to hide it somewhere but we couldn't just walk into a bank with it or ask Mum or Dad to, so how about burying it here?*

I see what you mean but what if someone – or a bat, say – saw us doing it. It could be dug up again. And what if Odric can somehow wake up without it? Aristotle says it's needed to defeat him – whatever that means.

The more they thought about it the more they realised that Aristotle's plan was right.

So the next evening Olly with Tilly beside him used the phone in the sitting room while their mother and father were in the kitchen. Their grandparents might have thought it odd if he used his mobile and anyway he did not want to use up his credit. Luckily Grandpa answered the phone.

'I thought one of you might ring,' he said. 'I bumped

into the Colonel this morning and he asked if you were coming over this weekend, as though he was half expecting you. Did Tilly make arrangements with him when she was over here last weekend? She didn't say anything to Granny or me about it.'

Loud alarm bells rang in Olly's head. The Colonel half expecting them!

'Not that I know of,' he said, trying to keep his voice on an even keel.

Tilly looked at him quizzically and he mouthed 'The Colonel' to her.

'But Mum and Dad are still painting the kitchen and we really ought to bring the Stone back.'

There was short silence at the other end.

'I see…' said Grandpa. 'The Stone. Hmm, I didn't think it would be needed quite so soon. Put me on to your mother. I'll see if she'll let you come over. Granny and I always like having you here.'

Olly heaved a sigh of relief.

'Thanks a lot Grandpa. We'll be very good and tidy and help with washing up and everything.'

'Unless you have more important things to do.'

Olly went to fetch his mother.

'I didn't hear the phone ring,' she said as Olly handed her the phone.

'Didn't you?' he answered vaguely.

When she came off the phone she said, 'Grandpa says he's asked both of you to go over to help them with the Antiques and Collectors Fair at the weekend. It's fine by me if you want to go. Dad and I have plenty on our hands, what with the decorating.'

'Well, I don't mind going,' said Olly, trying not to raise suspicion by sounding too keen.

'Same here,' said Tilly.

So it was settled.

What was that about the Colonel? Tilly asked when they were alone again touching the Stone.

When she heard she was as concerned as Olly.

It may be no accident that he bumped into Grandpa, she said, *because if he's an enemy it's a good way of finding out our plans and if he isn't an enemy what's he doing asking about us anyway?*

It may just have been a chance meeting and polite conversation, said Olly but on thinking about it they both realised that the Colonel was not one for polite conversation. Also they both agreed that Grandpa had reacted as though he knew more than he had told them.

We'd better ring Daniel and Kiran.

Tilly checked on what her parents were doing. They were talking at the table in the kitchen after finishing their tea. Olly kept his ear cocked in case they moved, while Tilly dialled the Akrams. Daniel answered.

'About time you rang,' he said before Tilly could get a word in. His words came out in a torrent. 'We've been waiting and waiting and waiting and waiting. I even tried to ring you a few minutes ago and your line was busy. I suppose you've been ringing all your friends to tell them what's going on and we're the last to know. Here we are with enemies all round probably and no news...'

'Daniel,' interrupted Tilly loudly.

'Yes?'

'Shut up and I'll tell you.'

'Oh, alright,' he said meekly.

'No-one but you and Kiran must know what I'm going to tell you, ok?'

'Yes,' he said excitedly. 'Just a minute, Kiran's going to pick up the extension in Mum and Dad's bedroom.' They heard her crashing up the stairs and a moment later she came on the line.

Tilly recounted all that had happened.

'Are you seriously telling me that you two can read

each other's thoughts?' Kiran asked.

'Yes. Olly's listening to you through me right now.' Tilly was holding the Stone.

'If it's true, he can prove it by burping down the phone without you asking him to,' said Daniel. He admired Olly's ability to burp at will. Olly obliged – loudly.

There was laughter from the other end.

'Is anything happening over there?' Tilly asked.

Daniel was still in torrential talking mode.

'I'm keeping a close eye on the Boyle sisters. I went into the shop after school today and they're still as creepy as ever. I wish you were here with the Stone because Jess, oh yes, I forgot to tell you that she was with me, started sniffing and scratching at the floor as though she was trying to dig it up and the Boyle sisters looked like thunder and the cat hissed and I'm sure it said something to Jess that made her angry so she started barking and altogether it was a bit of a scene and I had to rush out of the shop with Jess to calm things down and the sisters came to the door and gave me the dead-eye and then Jess was trying to tell me something – I'm sure she was.'

'She must have sniffed out where the trap door is,' said Kiran.

'I'm sure the Boyle sisters are enemies,' said Tilly, 'so keep away from the shop until we get there and don't go anywhere alone especially after dark. Watch out for the Colonel too. We still don't know where he stands.'

She told Daniel and Kiran what Grandpa had said about the Colonel.

'The sooner you get here, the better,' said Kiran. 'We need to have a serious talk with Jess to see if she's found anything out.'

'OK, see you Saturday. Watch out for bats, the Boyles

and any strange goings on. Also, if you see any mice, they're probably on our side.'

**

At around the same time the Colonel was brooding by the fire in his living room behind the shop. A beep from a computer on the corner table announced the arrival of an email. He read it and smiled grimly. The news was good as far as it went but he knew what he had to do.

12

HELLO DANIELL…

On Thursday morning the Boyles were looking out of their shop as Daniel and Kiran passed on their way to school. Their cold eyes met the children's and their mouths smiled. Late that afternoon on their way home both children thought they heard frigid laughter as they passed, which made them dash for their own front door.

'At least we're safe here,' said Kiran, once inside, 'and there'll be more of us once the Petersons get here.'

That night a storm blew up. First came freezing wind, light at first but getting stronger until it turned into a gale. Then driving rain, so cold it felt like pellets of ice. The sea produced mountainous waves that crashed heavily against the sea wall below the Akram's house. The outsides of the windows were coated with salt spray and inside it felt as though the foundations were shaking. The wind blew straight up the Dock and older villagers warned that when high tide came, around two a.m., the sea might flood the lower part of the road. It had happened before but only rarely. Some of the householders and shopkeepers near the Dock protected their doors with sandbags.

Fortunately the Akram's front door was well above the likely water level but just the same Mr Akram warned his family against going outside. It was all too easy to be swept away in such conditions.

So Kiran and Daniel stayed in, cosy in front of the living room fire until they went to bed.

Shortly after two o'clock Daniel stirred and opened his eyes. The storm was at its height and he could hear the roaring of wind and sea outside. It must have woken me, he thought. Then there was a sound in the room – a book falling from the bookcase. In the darkness he thought he could make out some movement and sensed a cold draught on his face. It had a damp, unfamiliar smell. He felt a stab of fear.

'Kiran, is that you?' he said quietly, his voice shaking a little. There was no reply. He put on the bedside light – and his heart stopped. One end of the bookcase had swung away from the wall like a door, to reveal a dark opening. Advancing from it towards him were the Boyle sisters.

'Hello, Danielll,' they whispered in chilling unison.

Daniel tried to shout but his voice had gone. Before he could make a sound the sisters were upon him. Astrid grabbed his head, stuffed a piece of cloth in his mouth and put sticky tape over it. Ingrid grabbed his arms and quickly tied them behind his back.

The cloth tasted foul in his mouth and made him choke. He wriggled and struggled, kicking his legs but they held him down. He got his voice back but, gagged as he was, the sound he made was drowned by the storm outside. They stood him up and dragged him, still struggling, towards the secret door, their bony fingers digging into his arms like talons. They gave off an unpleasant smell, somewhere between drains and rotting cauliflower. Within a few seconds he was out of the soft warm light of the bedroom and descending a cold dark stairway.

They stumbled down about 20 steps, with Daniel wriggling and kicking furiously. A tunnel ran past at the bottom and they turned left – towards the sea, Daniel thought. He collapsed his legs to make it more difficult for the sisters to drag him but the gritty stone floor grazed and hurt his bare feet. So in self-defence he tried to walk and pull back at the same time but that was almost as painful.

Astrid produced a small torch with a feeble light, as though the batteries were nearly flat. She and her sister pulled and pushed him about 200 metres along the tunnel and flung him to the ground. They tied his legs together and secured the free end of the rope to an iron ring in the wall. He had no option but to lie there on his back, shivering with fright and cold. The soles of his feet were painful with cuts and through his pyjamas he felt damp from the floor.

Ingrid and Astrid bent over him, grinning.

'We'll be back soonnn,' said Ingrid, 'be a gooood boy while we're gonnne.' The 'gooood' was long and sarcastic and came from somewhere inside her long nose.

They both walked quickly off into the darkness, back the way they had come. As they went he heard Astrid repeat 'gooood boy' in the same way that Ingrid had said it. They took it in turns to say it, sniggering coldly, until they were out of earshot.

It was pitch black when they had gone. Daniel was very frightened and on top of everything else was scared of something nasty creeping up on him from behind.. He tried to use his ears as eyes. Dripping water, distant sea thudding onto rocks. No sound of wind from the storm – he supposed they were too far underground to hear it – but what was that? He held his breath. Grit scraping lightly over the rock floor. Something was passing over it nearby. Not footsteps. Too light. Something sneaky and stealthy. Visions of snakes and slithering monsters with long fangs passed through his mind.

The sound came nearer. It was approaching from behind. He quelled an impulse to twist round and peer into the darkness. It would make too much noise – attract the monster towards him – and anyway, he thought, he wouldn't be able to see the monster unless it was carrying a torch which monsters usually don't and anyway it wasn't carrying one because he would have seen its light by now. So he lay there holding his breath, eyes wide with fear.

The sound was very near now. Whatever-it-was was almost upon him. He felt the lightest of touches on his shoulder. This is it, he thought. The next thing I feel will be teeth. He tried to cry out but the gag absorbed his voice. Then something small climbed onto his chest. There was a momentary flash of light that revealed a mouse holding a tiny torch. Daniel's whole body jumped with shock. The mouse leapt off into the darkness and was gone.

***

Back in Daniel's bedroom, Ingrid picked up his clothes and shoes where they had fallen when he undressed at bedtime. Astrid took his waterproof jacket from a hook on the back of the door and tiptoed silently onto the landing. There was no danger of being heard above the sound of the storm and Mr Akram's snoring. She crept downstairs, unlocked the front door and opened it a crack.

Outside it was just past high tide and, true to prediction, the sea boiled and foamed over the roadway below. She pushed her arm through the open door and threw Daniel's jacket into the water, watching with a satisfied smile as a wave caught it and swirled it away towards the open sea. Gently closing the door but not locking it, she rejoined her sister in the bedroom.

They left as they came, through the secret stone door to which the bookcase was attached, pulling it shut behind them. Despite the door's not having been used for centuries, its hinges were silent and it fit its opening precisely. Once closed it was impossible to tell that it was there.

***

Two a.m. saw *S.S. Dauntless* moored in the Leeds canal basin with steam up. Dauntless Arvicola had checked and re-checked everything a dozen times and was doing it again to make sure when Aristotle Badger arrived. His rucksack was larger than last time.

'All ready, my friend?' asked Aristotle.

'Y-Yes, sir.'

'Don't be nervous, now. Whatever happens we'll all cope together.'

'Y-yes, sir. That's just what d-dear Prudence said when we d-discussed it. I thought, sir, she would s-say that I shouldn't go but she d-didn't. She said, sir, that she was p-proud of me and although she didn't want me to be in any d-danger, she felt that if there was any I would be able to handle it, sir. I wish I f-felt as certain, sir. B-by the way, I hope you d-don't mind, sir but I said she could c-come with the b-babies to wave us off. They'll be at the p-private lock.'

The private lock was a small one, well camouflaged and unknown to humans. Dauntless Arvicola's father and grandfather had built it, to enable their ship to pass discreetly from the Leeds Liverpool Canal to the River Aire. Tonight *S.S. Dauntless* would sail down the river to the Humber. The shipping forecast was atrocious for the early part of the night but until they passed Spurn Point and turned northwards up the coast, they would be sheltered from the worst of it. Dauntless Arvicola hoped that the sea would have moderated a little by then.

As *S.S. Dauntless* moved smoothly into the lock, there on the bank, as arranged, was Prudence in her flowered hat and purple coat, standing with a large perambulator, bursting with babies. There had been just enough room in it for the four of them when they were newly born, sleeping head to tail, but they had grown since then and, excited at being up so late, were definitely not sleeping. As the ship sailed into the lock, they bounced up and down, waving and shouting, 'Daddy, daddy, daddy, daddy!'

Dauntless Arvicola and Aristotle waved and smiled and so did Prudence. Dauntless Arvicola pressed his remote control (a recent innovation) to close the lock gate behind them and to start hidden machinery that opened sluices, lowering the water level to that of the river. Then the outer lock gates opened and *S.S. Dauntless* passed through. Again, much waving and Prudence blew a kiss. She continued to wave until the ship was out of sight. Dauntless Arvicola kept looking back and waving too.

13

MEANWHISKER

Less than a minute after the mouse jumped off his chest, Daniel heard more soft movements, from the opposite direction this time. Two green eyes appeared in the darkness and stinking breath enveloped his face. The creature was obviously much bigger than a mouse. The teeth Daniel had previously expected must have arrived. He froze.

Then Meanwhisker gave a bad tempered miaow.

'Phew! What a relief,' thought Daniel, guessing who it was.

Meanwhisker was not happy. Earlier, Ingrid had sent her on another long errand underground. She didn't really mind these trips, because on the way back there were usually some tasty morsels to eat – after she had played with them – but tonight there was not a single mouse to be seen. It was unusually quiet, as though every creature down there was holding its breath. By the time she reached Daniel, she was tired, hungry – and bored. She needed some fun.

She sat down beside Daniel and sniffed. She could smell that her mistresses were nearby. She sniffed again. Apart from Daniel and Boyle, there was another more interesting smell, faint but clearly recognisable. Mouse. Perhaps things were looking up.

***

When Ian had arrived at Section H.Q. for the night shift, the report awaiting him of the sisters descending into the tunnel was already half an hour old. Nonetheless he had followed and first saw them as they were walking back towards the village after leaving something on the tunnel floor. Fortunately Ian was small enough for them not to notice him in the gloom. After discovering that the something was Daniel – who he had often seen in the village – and jumping off his chest, Ian ran back up the tunnel to see where the Boyles had gone.

After about 200 metres he saw light coming down some steps. He climbed to the top and, to his surprise, saw the door into Daniel's bedroom. Both Astrid and Ingrid were inside. He scampered down the steps and headed back towards Daniel. It would not take long to gnaw through the ropes.

It was so dark that to get his bearings he risked a quick flash of his torch, pointing down at the ground and shielding it with his hand. Big mistake. Up ahead, sitting beside Daniel, he saw the unmistakable outline of Meanwhisker and, with her keen night vision, Meanwhisker saw Ian. She leapt to her feet, already streaking towards him.

Ian ran for his life back up the tunnel, heart pumping at emergency speed. He could not release Daniel now but if he got out he could at least report what had happened. He headed straight for the telephone box entrance, a small hole in the tunnel roof too small for Meanwhisker, reached up a ladder of iron rungs in the wall. It would be touch and go. Meanwhisker was close behind and gaining but he thought he could make it.

Yes, there it was. He could see it because the telephone box was lit up and a chink of light came through the hole. Quick, up the ladder. Meanwhisker was right on his tail. Ian climbed at high speed but near the top slipped and fell back a rung.

That was all Meanwhisker needed. She swiped him with a paw. A claw penetrated Ian's back and he cried out in pain. Meanwhisker smiled. This was going to be fun. She withdrew the claw but only to get a better grip and at the second blow three sharp claws went in deep. Ian shrieked in agony.

So near to freedom, yet so far. Less than a tail's length. But he was so badly wounded, he could not make it. He felt waves of pain and his grip on the rungs slackened. Meanwhisker chuckled. She could sense Ian failing. Already she was anticipating a tasty meal but first she would play. She climbed up a rung to get a better hold on him. Ian's pain redoubled as the claws flexed, penetrating vital organs. He felt blood pumping out of his wounds.

If only he could get to the hole. He looked up at it longingly, desperate to make the effort to get there but unable to do so. It might as well have been a mile away. Then, a shadow seemed to pass across it. A moving shadow. There was something there in the hole and it was making a sound. What was it? The sound was familiar but pain was blocking his memory.

He felt numbness creeping up from his feet and started to feel cold. But the sound went on.

Suddenly some last reserve of strength was released and he understood.

'Ian, Ian,' Liam was shouting from the hole, 'listen, listen. When I shout *now*, climb the last rung. When I shout *now*, climb the last rung.' At the same time Liam pressed the emergency button just inside the trap door opening, flashing a distress message to H.Q. Medical Centre.

Ian smiled. How easy it sounded, yet Liam might have asked him to climb a mountain. He was too tired.

Liam, looking down on the two creatures, took careful aim with his catpin and hurled it with all his might at Meanwhisker's head. The cat screeched, clapped a paw to her nose and released her grip on Ian. In doing so she lost her balance, swayed and teetered then fell, still screeching.

'*Now*, Ian, now, now, *now!*' shouted Liam at the top of his voice.

Ian was only just conscious. Slowly, as though his whole body weighed a ton, he painfully raised himself up one more rung so that his hands were now on the top one. Liam was leaning through the hole, stretching out to him. But Ian had no more strength. He could go no further. He feebly raised a hand to wave goodbye and felt himself falling into a dark abyss.

The raised hand was all Liam needed. He grabbed it just as Ian went limp, and with strength he did not know he had, he hauled Ian up through the hole.

'Phew, you had me worried,' said Liam but Ian did not respond. He lay on the ground not moving, covered in blood from the neck down. Now realising the severity of Ian's injuries, Liam knelt beside his friend and took his hand.

'Hang in there, Ian,' he said, 'help's on the way. Don't conk out on me. We've a lot to do yet.' But he could feel no pulse, no sign of life. As the stretcher-bearers arrived, tears began to roll down Liam's face.

14

BOTWULF

Daniel had no idea why Meanwhisker ran off but the mouse-on-the-chest episode had given him hope and he was able to think more rationally about his plight. The word from Tilly had been that mice were good. With any luck that mouse would get out and alert someone to where he was. He began to hum as his spirits rose a little.

'Gooood boy, humming,' said Ingrid. The sisters had returned so quietly that his humming had drowned the sound.

'Hummmingngng,' repeated Astrid nasally, prolonging the word until sounded like a wasp.

'Mm, hummmingngng,' they both chuntered.

Daniel stopped humming. He did not want them to suspect that anything had happened while they had been away.

'Gooood boy, get dresssed,' said Astrid. She dropped the bundle of clothes beside him and began to untie his hands and feet.

'Gooood boy, don't try to run away,' said Ingrid. 'Nowhere to runnn. Dark tunnnellls. Lurking dannngerrr.'

'Nowhere to runnn,' repeated Astrid.

Daniel was fed up with their dismal talk and had every intention of running back up the tunnel as soon as he got his shoes and socks on. Lurking danger there might be but he was willing to take a chance.

He quickly pulled on his clothes, over his pyjamas for warmth, and was just reaching for his shoes and socks, when Astrid slipped a noose of rope over his head and knotted it round his neck, loose enough for him to breathe but tight enough not to slip off. Daniel cursed to himself, disappointed.

After he had put on his shoes, Astrid tied his hands behind his back again. His legs were free so he could walk or even run but he was unable to go anywhere that the sisters did not want.

They heard a miaow and Meanwhisker sauntered into the circle of dim light from Astrid's torch. Ingrid knelt to stroke her and Daniel heard them making quiet cat-noises to one another. It sounded like they were having a conversation.

Meanwhisker was feeling somewhat deflated by the indignity of her recent fall and her nose was stinging badly from Liam's catpin. In Cat Ingrid asked her if she had any message from below.

'Yes,' said Meanwhisker, 'he said first the boy is to be brought down to him and then he has a note for you to deliver.'

'Good, gooddd,' said Ingrid in Cat. 'Well done, my little queen. And did you find a tasty mousey?'

'Yes, mistress, just a few minutes ago,' Meanwhisker lied, not wanting to admit that she had let one get away. 'Very tasty.'

'Clever, clever,' said Ingrid, stroking her some more. 'Now my little queen can go home.'

Meanwhisker strolled off.

'We take the boy downnn,' said Ingrid to Astrid. 'Then a note to deliverrr.'

Daniel pricked up his ears.

'Little queen caught a tasty mousey,' added Ingrid, almost salivating.

'Tasty mousey,' repeated Astrid, with a sinister giggle. 'Taaasssty mousey.'

If it had not been for the gag, Daniel would have

cried out. Meanwhisker had caught the mouse! Now no one would know where he was. Suddenly the hope he had dared to feel was dashed. He would be just one more missing person, an anonymous statistic in police records. People would assume he had run away to London to take drugs. They would shake their heads in the post office and the village store and ask, 'What have Mr and Mrs Akram done to deserve this? What a silly boy Daniel must be.' While all the time he was being held prisoner underground. If he was lucky. What if he wasn't lucky? He dared not think about it.

Tears were forcing their way out of his eyes. He tried to swallow a sob but swallowed some of the gag instead, which made him retch and cough. In turn, that made him want to inhale more deeply but the gag prevented it. He fell to the ground choking.

None too quickly or gently, Astrid ripped the sticky tape off his mouth. He spat out the cloth gag, gasping. Ignoring the stinging pain where the sticky tape had been pulled off, he filled his lungs and yelled at the top of his voice. The yell was not words; it was just a wail but it expressed all his feelings of fear and desolation. It did not bother Ingrid and Astrid. They were too far underground for anyone to hear. They just snickered to each other. As they marched him off, the rope round his neck like a lead on a pet dog, Daniel realised the hopelessness of his position and fell into a gloomy silence.

Further and further they went. There were many forks in the tunnel and despite the darkness the sisters always seemed to know which branch to take. Like others before him Daniel gradually realised that the chosen route was always downwards.

All the time the sisters chittered and murmured to each other. He gave up trying to tell what they said. If one said something the other usually repeated it and they tossed it backwards and forwards between them, saying it again and again until it jarred on his nerves.

Eventually the little party came to a halt. The tunnel continued ahead but on their right was a heavy door, slightly ajar. Ingrid and Astrid pulled Daniel through it into a short passage. At the end was another door and before it some stone steps leading down to the left. For once they did not take the downward direction. Ingrid knocked gently on the second door and opened it without waiting for a response. Light streamed out of the door, not bright by normal standards but in contrast to the gloom elsewhere it seemed like a spotlight.

As they entered, blinking, they were greeted by a voice that sounded as though it came from the depths of winter. It scraped and grated like fingernails on a blackboard, putting Daniel's teeth on edge

'Welcome, sisters,' said the voice, 'you have done well. You will be rewarded when our master rises.'

The sisters smirked and simpered.

Although the words were of welcome and praise, the voice was so cold that it sounded to Daniel more like a death sentence. He shivered and felt bleaker than ever.

The light came from an oil lamp on a table strewn with papers. There were chairs round the table but the lit part of the room was otherwise bare, as were the dark walls. Daniel could not tell how large the room was or what might be beyond the lamp other than the voice.

The sisters pushed Daniel forward. Out of the shadows came a bent and ragged creature. Daniel could see that it was human, or at least once had been. If it had stood erect, its full height would have been that of a normal adult. As it was, the creature's hood, part of its black robe, was at the same level as Daniel's head. He could not see its face. Only a long hooked nose was visible beneath the hood, while skeletal hands protruded from the sleeves. They seemed to have no covering of flesh, just skin stretched over bone, every joint misshapen. The scraggy feet wore sandals.

This must be Botwulf, thought Daniel. Close up he was frightening and also gave off a stomach-churning body odour. The worst Daniel had ever come across, including from his own trainers, which was saying something.

'Phew!' he said, before he could stop himself. 'What a stink.'

Then he started to laugh. Just a chuckle at first but it grew and grew until he was more or less hysterical. He did not understand why – maybe it was fear or panic – but it was uncontrollable. He knew his captors would not like it but I've had it anyway, he thought.

The laughter obviously puzzled the Boyles who muttered disapprovingly to each other. Botwulf appeared not to react until he raised a bony hand towards Daniel.

'Silence!' he croaked loudly, to no avail.

The Boyle sisters became quiet and shifted their feet nervously.

As Daniel's hysteria started to subside he noticed that in the confusion Astrid had loosened her grip on the other end of the rope. If she was caught unawares, a good pull might slip it out of her hand. But his hands were still tied behind his back. To give himself time to think, he continued laughing longer than he needed to. Then in one quick movement he dived for the door and the rope was yanked out of Astrid's hand.

He was along the short passage and turning up the main tunnel towards the village before the sisters and Botwulf could stop him, rope trailing behind. He knew the chance of escape was slim but he had to have a go.

Stumbling and tripping in the darkness, he did not

know if he could outrun the Boyles – they had longer legs – but he had youth and lots of football practice on his side. He would give them a run for their money. Botwulf did not look as though he could run far. Listening as he ran he could hear nothing behind him. Surely they must be after him. He risked slowing down to listen harder. No, nothing. He redoubled his pace. They might not be following now but they could at any minute and what about the lurking danger Ingrid had threatened. Speed was obviously essential.

Back in Botwulf's room, Astrid had at first been shocked, then ashamed at letting go of the rope. She was also frightened that Botwulf might punish her. She shrieked in horror and set off to give chase with Ingrid right behind but Botwulf again held up his hand.

'Stop, sisters, stop!' he croaked. 'You were foolish to drop your guard but I anticipated the possibility of something like this. Nothing will stop our plan.'

He glided to the gloomy back of the room and the sisters followed. Beside another door two levers protruded from the wall and Botwulf took hold of one of them.

'Silence, while I listen,' he said. 'My ears have become sharper with the passing years.'

The three of them fell silent while Botwulf listened to the sound of Daniel running up the passage. Daniel was not exactly trying to be quiet but the sisters could not hear him.

Then Botwulf pulled down the lever.

'There,' he rasped, 'our guest is in the pit.'

'The pittt,' the sisters chortled to each other, 'the pittt.' Then, looking into each other's eyes as though the realisation of some great truth was dawning, they spoke in unison, almost a chant: 'Curwald, Curwald, Curwald...'

Just as Daniel began to feel he might get away he ran

off a cliff. His legs continued running as his brain struggled to grasp what was going on. It seemed to happen in slow motion. His hands were still tied so he could not protect himself.

Thud! His feet and knees hit the bottom.

Thud! His chest.

Thud! His forehead.

He cried out in pain and lay there face down as a wave of nausea swept over him. He felt he was going to pass out. He gritted his teeth and told himself to stay conscious.

After a while the pain became less and he turned over to sit up. Nothing was broken as far as he could tell but his head ached badly. Blood was streaming into his right eye, making it sting, then running down his cheek. His knees hurt and were sticking to the pyjamas inside his jeans so he assumed they were bleeding too.

He stumbled to his feet and strained his eyes to make out what he could of his new surroundings. Total blackness above yet with a faint hint of light from Botwulf's room, just enough to outline dimly the rectangular opening he had fallen down.

I wonder why we didn't see it on our way down from the village, he thought.

The answer to his question came immediately. As Botwulf moved the lever again, a section of the tunnel floor slid back into place blocking out further light. Daniel was now in darkness so deep that he could not tell whether his eyes were open or shut.

He stood stock still with his back to the wall and listened intently. Complete silence apart from his own breathing. He held his breath. Nothing apart from the beating of his heart. He could not stop that. Alright, he thought, at least it sounds as though there's nothing here to pounce on me. Let's see if I can get out.

Carefully, he began to edge along the wall, his back to it so that he could touch the damp rock with his bound hands. In a few moments he came into a corner. He edged round it and along the next wall. Soon there was another corner. About half way along the third wall there was a gap not much more than a metre wide. He took a few steps into it, listening hard. No sound but a nasty smell like bad eggs and rotting fish. Well, he thought, I'd better see if there are any other gaps that smell better. He completed his circuit of the pit but found none.

It's the smelly route or nothing, he thought. Plucking up courage, he cautiously walked into it. Although he could not see the height of the passage, the small sounds he made as he walked did not echo and he sensed that the roof was quite close to his head.

***

Curwald the wolf was almost as old as Botwulf, whom he loved, hated and feared in equal measure. His memories of cubhood were now dim but he knew that he had been captured for the experiments of Odric and Botwulf. Initially he had resisted, for he was physically strong, but eventually he succumbed to merciless mental attack. Odric had first destroyed Curwald's mind with early prototypes of the Stone then rebuilt it to his own specification – evil, cruel and cunning. When Edwin and Alfred had released the captive creatures Curwald had not wished to go back to the surface. He stayed underground, preferring the shadows.

Another effect of Odric's work was that Curwald's sleeping, eating and ageing rhythms slowed down. A year to him was close to a century for normal humans. A normal night's sleep lasted 2-3 months and a normal day the same length of time. For thirteen centuries Botwulf had nurtured and admired him in Odric's absence.

Curwald was uncontrollably aggressive and revelled in his own strength. Without conscience, he would turn on any living thing and tear it to pieces.

So dangerous was Curwald that even Botwulf dare not let him out of the pit. Now, as Daniel walked unknowingly down the tunnel towards his lair, Curwald stirred from sleep, opening his vicious red eyes. For him it was the start of a new day and he was hungry. He yawned, baring his yellow fangs and licking his chops. He wondered what morsels might come his way and what sport might be had in the kill. The scent of Daniel approaching reached him almost at the same moment as the sound. Immediately he was alert, sniffing appreciatively and listening. Good, he thought. His master had not failed him. A meal was approaching. He waited in silence ready to pounce.

***

The further Daniel walked in the darkness the worse the smell became. Once he thought he heard growling some distance ahead, as though from a large animal. He stopped to listen but heard nothing so continued. A few minutes later he sensed a curve in the tunnel and as he rounded it there was a mighty roar in the darkness right in front of him.

15

MISSING

Travelling to Scar Bay on Friday after school, Olly and Tilly were excited in a nervous kind of way and kept wondering if they would see Heron or Wickfeather flying past.

In Scarborough, as they were walking from the train to the bus, they noticed local newspaper headline boards:

BAY BOY FEARED DROWNED

'D'you think they mean Scar Bay?' Tilly asked.

'Could be. I hope it's no-one we know.'

They felt apprehensive and with daylight gone their mood seemed to darken but they were unprepared for the situation at Scar Bay when they stepped off the bus.

In the car park at the top of village were five police cars with blue lights flashing, a large police van labelled 'Mobile Incident Room', an ambulance and the yellow rescue helicopter. There were floodlights and the sound of a diesel generator. The hiss and chatter of radios was everywhere.

Despite strong wind, bitter cold and driving rain there were a lot of policemen and a crowd of familiar faces from the village, many in waterproofs and boots, some carrying torches. There were also camera crews and reporters.

As well as those already in the car park there were several small groups approaching up the steep hill from the Dock. They looked tired.

A Police Inspector, standing on the steps of the

Mobile Incident Room, began to speak through a loudspeaker.

'Ladies and Gentlemen,' he said, 'we're calling off the search for tonight. It's too dark now and the weather's too bad. To continue in these conditions would only endanger more people. Thank you all for your efforts today. Go home, have something to eat, get some sleep and we'll start again at first light tomorrow.'

Both grandparents were there. Granny looked as though she had been crying.

'What's happening?' asked Tilly.

'Daniel,' said Grandpa. He did not need to say any more. It was all too obvious.

'Oh no!' Tilly cried and tears started to flow. Olly felt his eyes water too. Both grandparents hugged them and none of them could speak for a few moments.

The searchers in the car park seemed reluctant to go home. They knew there was nothing more they could do that night but they desperately wanted to do something. In the middle of them were Mr and Mrs Akram with Kiran. The children could tell they had been crying too, even Mr Akram, but they were being very brave and thanking everyone. In return they received words of encouragement about more searching tomorrow.

The appearance of the Peterson children set Mrs Akram and Kiran off crying again.

'What happened?' asked Olly. Kiran explained.

'There was a bad storm last night and this morning Daniel wasn't in his bed. His pyjamas and clothes were gone and we couldn't find him. The front door was unlocked and Dad's quite certain he locked it last night. In fact, Mum says she saw him do it. At first we thought he'd just gone out early to see if the high tide had done any damage,' her voice quivered 'but the Colonel was walking on the beach with Jess first thing this morning and found Daniel's jacket washed up near Doggle Hole. So we called the police and they called the coastguard, who called out the rescue helicopter and the search teams and they all think Daniel's been swept out to sea by the storm. He must have gone out in the middle of the night. Oh, why…Oh de-e-e-ar,' and she broke down into sobbing again.

Olly and Tilly did not know what to say. It was too awful to say anything so they just hugged Kiran and her parents. It did not stop them thinking things though.

So the Colonel found his jacket.

Eventually the Akrams, the Petersons and all the searchers turned reluctantly for home. The Colonel and Jess appeared out of the darkness. They both looked wet and tired. They had been searching all day.

'Very sorry,' said the Colonel to the Akrams. 'No result yet. Chin up. Try again tomorrow. Bound to find him. Tough young lad. Do all I can.'

Mr Akram thanked him and they all moved off down the hill. They hoped the Colonel was right about finding Daniel but if he had not been found by this time, there must be doubt about whether he could survive the night in such conditions.

Olly had the Stone in his pocket. He and Tilly hung back a little with Jess, bending to stroke her and tickle her ears. 'Hello Jess,' said Olly, 'you must be tired.' He thought he'd better say something ordinary in case anyone was listening.

'Certainly am,' replied Jess. 'And what a relief to be able to talk to you. I bet you're thinking the Colonel had something to do with Daniel's disappearance – just because we found the jacket. Well, the Colonel was at home all night last night and was just as surprised as I was to find it. In fact he was very upset, I could tell. So am I, come to that.'

The children stroked her consolingly and all three agreed how awful it was.

The Colonel was striding off home and Jess was straining to follow.

'Have a good feed and a sleep. We'll talk to you in the morning,' said Olly. 'Daniel told us what happened in the Boyles' shop and we've a lot to tell you, including that there are steps to an underground passage under that flagstone in the shop.'

'I knew it,' said Jess triumphantly. 'And those bloomin' Boyle sisters haven't been helping to search either. See you tomorrow.'

Back in the warmth of the grandparent's cottage, the awful truth about Daniel started to sink in and the atmosphere was rather sombre. Granny quickly made their tea but all four appetites had gone away.

'I think we should cancel the Antiques and Collectors Fair, don't you, Bill?' asked Granny.

'Definitely,' Grandpa agreed. 'We wouldn't be able to concentrate on it for thinking about Daniel. And virtually the whole village will be out searching anyway. With something like this you can't just carry on as though nothing has happened.'

'We'll help with the search, too,' said Olly.

Both children found it difficult to get to sleep. Lying in their warm beds in the snug bedroom over the kitchen, they thought of Daniel struggling in icy water, or shivering on a windswept beach. And that was the best they could hope for. The worst was just too awful to think about.

'We were expecting something strange and probably awful to happen this weekend,' said Olly, 'but never this.'

As he said it a thought struck them both. Tilly voiced it first.

'Well, if we didn't know what to expect, why are we

surprised at Daniel disappearing?'

They both thought about this for a moment.

'So, maybe it's connected with the Stone business.' said Olly. 'You heard what Jess said about the Boyle sisters not helping with the search. Maybe they've got something to do with Daniel going missing. I wonder if Heron knows anything or if Aristotle has arrived. The mice might have picked something up.'

16

CONTACT

About half past one in the morning Olly was woken by a gentle tap on his shoulder. Light from the staircase filtered under the bedroom door so he could easily see the mouse on his pillow. It wore glasses with thick lenses. Remembering all Aristotle had said about the mice, he was careful not to startle – or underestimate – it. Obviously it was there for a reason. Avoiding sudden movements, he reached for the Stone, at the same time whispering to Tilly to wake up. She stirred but remained asleep. When he held the Stone, Olly quietly asked the mouse a question.

'Do you want to talk?'

'Yes,' said the mouse. 'My name's Liam.'

'OK,' said Olly, getting out of bed. He asked Liam if it was alright to pick him up. Liam sensed he would be safe in Olly's hand so he said yes. Olly crossed to Tilly's bed and shook her shoulder. She was instantly awake.

Olly sat on the edge of her bed and they both touched the Stone. Liam sat between them.

'We need your help, urgently,' he said. 'I've come at Wickfeather's suggestion.'

'Just tell us and we'll do it,' said Olly. Tilly nodded her agreement.

'Our Section Leader Ian was dreadfully wounded last night by Meanwhisker, the Boyles' cat. Such terrible injuries would have killed most mice. He's had an emergency operation but the doctor's only giving him a fifty percent chance of survival.' Liam's voice wavered and his eyes filled with tears.

'We've heard of Ian,' said Olly. 'A brave mouse.'

'Yes,' said Liam, 'and my greatest friend. The thing is, Meanwhisker caught Ian in the tunnels and we think he may have discovered something very important beforehand. He went down there because our surveillance team at the Boyles' shop reported that the two sisters had gone down the tunnels which they have never done before as far as we know. But now Ian can't tell us what he saw. Wickfeather wondered if you and the Stone might be able to read his mind, even though he's unconscious.'

The children did not know if they could but neither hesitated.

'We can try,' said Olly.

They dressed and crept downstairs. The grandparents were snoring. Outside they carried Liam so they could move faster. He sat in Olly's coat pocket with his head poking out.

'We're going to Section H.Q.,' said Liam. 'It's on King Street.'

King Street used to be the main road into the village but hundreds of years ago it had collapsed into the sea, apart from a short section near the Dock.

The quickest way to it was along several back streets and alleys. Sensing the urgency, the children ran, taking care not to make too much noise.

'Left at the post box,' said Liam. There was a steep cobbled alley running a short distance from King Street to the sea wall. Halfway along Liam said, 'Here.' As they stopped, Liam climbed out of Olly's pocket and with great agility ran down his leg to the ground. There was a square metal drain cover with a small hole at one corner. Liam disappeared down it.

Machinery whirred and the drain cover hinged open to reveal Liam, beckoning, at the top of a flight of steps.

Following him down, they reached an underground corridor, just high enough for them, with wall lights and a number of closed doors. Liam ran under one of them so the children tried the handle and went in.

It was obviously a sick bay. There were six beds of varying size, none of them big enough for a person, together with cabinets of surgical instruments, dressings, bottles of medicine and pills. All the beds were empty except for the smallest one at the far end of the room. Standing beside it was Wickfeather, a rabbit in a white coat with a stethoscope round its neck and a mouse in nurse's uniform. In the bed lay Ian with many tubes and wires connecting him to medical equipment.

Wickfeather greeted the children warmly, introducing them to Dr Quick and Nurse Elaine.

'I'm afraid Ian's condition is serious,' said Dr Quick solemnly. 'Frankly, I don't know if he will survive. The next half hour will be critical.'

Nurse Elaine sniffled.

'Has he spoken?' asked Tilly.

'No,' said Dr Quick. 'His heart had stopped when the stretcher bearers brought him in. We used the defibrillator to start him up again and operated to repair the worst of the damage but he's remained unconscious. Fortunately, it's less than a hundred metres from the telephone box to here so we were able to get at him quickly. It's unlikely there's any brain damage.'

'Is that where Meanwhisker got him?' asked Olly. 'The telephone box?'

'Well, below it, actually,' said Wickfeather. 'It's only thanks to Liam's daring rescue that Ian got out at all.'

Liam looked embarrassed.

'Shall we try the Stone now?' asked Olly.

'As soon as you like,' said Wickfeather.

'If you can communicate with him at all,' said Nurse

Elaine, 'tell him we all love him and want him back.'

A tear trickled down her cheek.

'Right,' said Olly, turning to his sister. 'We'd better do this together.'

They knelt down beside the bed, both touching the Stone with one hand. Ian looked very small and frail.

'Can you hear me, Ian?' asked Olly but there was no reply. Tilly tried with the same result. They began to lose hope.

'He might hear better if we touch him,' suggested Tilly. Very gently they each placed a forefinger at either side of his head, the least injured part of him, and closed their eyes.

'Can you hear me Ian?' asked Olly again.

Both children felt a rush of fear and they were running for all they were worth along a dark tunnel. Meanwhisker was behind them. They spotted rungs in the wall and raced up them but slipped near the top. Then they felt a searing pain in the back and both of them cried out, losing their grip on the Stone.

The room came back into focus. The pain disappeared.

'Wow,' said Olly. 'I think we made contact!'

They recounted what had happened. 'Ian's mind must be re-running the last few minutes before his injury,' said Tilly.

'We'll never get anywhere unless we can get him to calm down,' said Olly. 'Let's have another go but this time try not to be carried along by his stream of thought.'

Again they closed their eyes, touching the Stone and Ian's temples.

The same rush but this time they stood their ground, telling themselves it was an illusion, like having a dream whilst wide awake. It worked. They were standing knee deep in an underground river with Ian's thoughts rushing past like a torrent of water. Their bodies felt light but they were not being swept away.

'Ian,' said Olly gently, 'listen to me. You're safe now.' The flow of the river slowed. 'Yes, that's it,' he went on, 'you can slow down and relax. Meanwhisker has gone and you're among friends. I'm Olly Peterson and my sister Tilly is here too.'

Nurse Elaine wiped away a tear.

The river slowed and narrowed a little. It was no longer underground. There was sunlight and blue sky.

Dr Quick looked worried. 'His pulse is getting weaker,' he said, looking at the monitoring equipment. The children could hear and understand but with their eyes closed they were seeing a different world. Sitting on a stone on the other side of the river was a mouse they both knew was Ian. Somehow they also knew that speech was not now necessary for communication.

Won't you come over to this side and sit with us, asked Tilly

I can't, said Ian, *because of my injuries.* Suddenly, he was further away. *Can you help me? I have some important information but not enough time to tell you it.*

Go after him, Olly, said Tilly. *I'll stay here in case you need help to come back.* Instinctively, they knew that it would be difficult to come back, that few who crossed could return.

Olly waded vigorously across. Ian moved yet further away.

'His blood pressure's taken a dive,' said Dr Quick, frowning.

Olly caught up with Ian. Although Tilly was back on the other side their minds were together, a pooled resource of energy.

Let me help you back, said Olly.

I don't know if I have the strength, Ian replied. *I want to tell*

you about Daniel though.

As he did so his voice gradually weakened.

'I think we're losing him,' said Dr Quick.

Nurse Elaine took hold of Ian's hand.

Olly looked over his shoulder and the river was further away now. Ian's eyes had closed and he seemed to be asleep.

We've got to do something, Tilly sent. *Bring him back here.*

Olly tried to lift him but he could not. It seemed that the injuries added weight to Ian's body, and a force like gravity was both holding him down and pulling him away from the river.

Yet each of the children felt a strong desire – almost a need – to help, and their joined minds responded by trying to find a way. Eyes still firmly closed they were able on a mental level to look inside Ian and in a few seconds they saw what all his injuries were. Then they were able to visualise how Ian's body would be if the injuries had never happened and they longed with great intensity for him to return to that state. One by one the injuries seemed to disappear and they knew that he was being healed.

When they had done it Olly again tried to pick Ian up and this time he was his normal weight. Olly ran with him to the river bank and walked into the water. It felt heavy and the current was against him. He shouted to Tilly but she knew already. She stepped into the water intending to grab them and pull them back but at once the joined minds became aware of how to soothe and reduce the flow so that it parted more easily for Olly and Ian to cross. Soon she was helping them out onto the grassy bank.

Dr Quick could not believe his eyes as he surveyed the monitors.

'Heart rate rising… blood pressure rising….'

Then a moment later:

'Heart rate stable and regular…vital signs normal!'

Olly and Tilly removed their fingers from Ian's temples and opened their eyes. The real world again.

Ian stirred and everyone leaned over the bed, Liam at the front. Ian opened his eyes

'Hello, Liam,' he said, still weak but smiling. 'I feel like something to eat.'

'You nearly were,' said Liam, tears of relief running down his face and they all laughed.

'It's a miracle,' said Nurse Elaine. Ian squeezed her hand and she blushed.

'My mind was stuck in a groove, running up that tunnel,' said Ian, 'then I heard a very calm voice telling me I was safe and I just knew to trust it, so I stopped running. Then Olly and Tilly appeared and…here I am!'

Olly and Tilly felt drained yet excited but were not able to explain what they had done. They just knew it was amazing and that it had happened instinctively. Wickfeather was in no doubt.

'What we have seen here tonight is part of the gift left to us by Alfred. We know that he used the Stone to heal and now we have proof that his descendants can do it too.'

As he was speaking the door opened and in walked Aristotle Badger followed closely by Dauntless Arvicola. They had just disembarked from *S.S. Dauntless*, having sailed in on the high tide. The ship was concealed at the mouth of a tunnel near the Dock, where a fresh water stream ran into the bay.

'Proof, you say?' Aristotle questioned.

Wickfeather recounted the dramatic events.

'Proof indeed,' replied Aristotle, smiling warmly.

'If you're not too tired,' Tilly said to Ian, 'we'd really like to know what you found out about Daniel.' There was a murmur of agreement.

Ian pushed himself up on one elbow. He told them about finding Daniel tied up, the secret entrance to his bedroom, the Boyle sisters and the pursuit by Meanwhisker. Everyone was astonished.

'I'm just so sorry that I wasn't able to free Daniel,' he said

'You did well, nonetheless,' said Wickfeather. 'Now, at least, we know that Daniel was alive last night.'

Everyone was relieved but Tilly was thoughtful.

'Anything could have happened since then, though,' she said quietly.

She did not say what she meant by 'anything'. Everyone understood the awful possibilities.

'But,' Olly responded immediately, 'why would anyone go to the trouble of tying him up and taking him down the tunnel if they really intended to do something worse?'

'Good point,' said Aristotle. 'I think the world is intended to think that Daniel has been swept away but really he has been kidnapped for some other purpose. What that is we can only speculate.'

'Now,' said Dr Quick, 'this is all very interesting but in the interests of my patient I must ask you all to leave. He may have been the subject of a miracle but he still needs rest.'

Ian was, indeed, looking pale and tired.

'You are quite right,' said Wickfeather, 'and the rest of us have also had a tiring night, particularly the young humans. It is now three a.m. May I suggest that we all get some rest and meet here again tomorrow at nine. We have much to discuss.'

'But what about Daniel?' asked Tilly.

'Naturally,' said Aristotle, 'our thoughts turn to rescue but we will not be effective in making a plan or implementing if we are all exhausted. Besides, there may be more information from the surveillance teams tomorrow.'

Reluctantly, everyone prepared to leave.

'I'll stay and look after Ian,' said Nurse Elaine happily.

'Just one more thing,' said Aristotle, leading a rather windswept vole to the front of the group. He had been hovering uncertainly by the door. 'I would like to introduce you all to Captain Dauntless Arvicola whose first class seamanship has brought me here tonight through very difficult weather conditions.'

The vole's nose went deep red with embarrassment.

17

A NOTE

The wind was still strong when Olly and Tilly left Section H.Q. to return to the cottage. It bent every tree and bush, causing shadows to dance and change in the light of the few old-fashioned streetlamps. Once Olly thought he saw a different kind of shadow wheeling and flitting at the edge of the darkness. He was not mistaken. Wartwing and his friends were out in force, to gather what information they could.

To the children's dismay a light showed through the living-room curtains at the cottage and when they went in they found Grandpa sitting in his dressing gown by the embers of the fire. Now we're for it, they thought.

'Ah, there you are,' he said affably. 'I thought I heard someone on the stairs earlier so I got up to investigate.'

'Er, hello Grandpa,' said Tilly hesitantly. The children's minds were racing to find a plausible explanation for being out in the middle of the night.

'We were just... ' Olly began. He had not thought of an excuse. He just hoped something would come into his mind. Grandpa interrupted in a low voice.

'Look, I don't know where you've been and I don't want you to make up any silly explanations. I know you both well enough to be sure you've been out for some good reason and if you're able to tell me you will. I'd hazard a guess that it's something to do with the Stone, which makes it important and probably too complicated to explain in a short time at this hour of the night. I won't interfere but your Granny won't share my views so it's important she doesn't know what's going on. In fact, the fewer people who know the better. Just remember – if you think I can help I'll do my best.'

The children were taken by surprise. They both thought how different their parents' attitude would have been. Grandpa actually gave them credit for being sensible and thinking for themselves. Their parents would have been too busy lecturing them to think about the real issues.

'It *is* to do with the Stone,' said Olly, 'and we'll tell you all about it tomorrow but we have an appointment in the village at nine o'clock so it can't be until after that. We can say, though, that Daniel may not have fallen into the sea and may be held prisoner but I don't think we can tell Mr and Mrs Akram or the police yet because it would mean too much explaining.'

'That's good news,' said Grandpa, 'or at least not quite such bad news as if Daniel had fallen into the sea but it does mean that he's probably in danger and you two may be too. So keep a sharp lookout and I'll try to keep an eye on you as well. Now, no more talk. Up to bed.'

They tiptoed upstairs. Luckily Granny was still snoring.

Next morning she had to shake the children to wake them.

'Goodness,' she scolded, 'wake up. I don't know what's got into everyone this morning. Grandpa's still in bed, too. No one would believe you've just had a night's sleep.'

Drowsy though the children were, they could not hold back a giggle.

Over breakfast the children could tell from the way Granny spoke that she doubted if Daniel could have survived the night but was avoiding saying it so as not to upset them.

'We just have to hope,' she said with a brave smile.

The children nodded to avoid being drawn into discussion.

'I feel so sorry for Mr and Mrs Akram and Kiran,' said Tilly. They could all agree with that.

Instead of the Antiques and Collectors Fair, Granny and Mrs Hutton were going to organise soup, sandwiches and tea in the village hall for the searchers and others involved. So after breakfast she put on her coat.

'You come too, Bill. We'll need you to put up trestle tables and lift the tea urn.'

'Right-o, dear. I'll be round as soon as I've arranged with these two what they're going to do.'

Just as Granny was leaving she remembered something.

'I'm in such a hurry I almost forgot to tell you. Before the three of you came downstairs the Colonel popped his head round the door and said he'd be pleased if you children would join the search with him and Jess, so I said that would be fine and he could keep an eye on you at the same time. He'll be at the car park at nine o'clock. You'd better get a move on – you've only got fifteen minutes.'

As Granny raced out of the door and slammed it behind her the children looked at each other in dismay. The Colonel again! Was he really as innocent as Jess believed? And they were due at Section H.Q. for nine.

'Don't worry,' said Grandpa. 'I'll nip up to the car park and tell the Colonel you're not ready and you'll catch up with him later.'

'Thank you, Grandpa,' said Olly, relieved. He did not add that they were not sure whose side the Colonel was on and that he might have an ulterior motive for wanting the children with him that day.

The Colonel's shop was shut when they went past on the way to Section H.Q. and they presumed he was already up at the car park. The Boyles' shop was open though, and there were one or two customers inside. At the back of the queue was a familiar tall figure with a Labrador.

'The Colonel!' said Tilly. 'Quick – hide.'

It was too late, they had been seen. The Colonel waved and Jess bounded out of the shop towards them. Tilly had the Stone in her pocket.

'He's buying humbugs,' said Jess. 'Are you coming to search with us?'

The children had no problem with Jess knowing the truth and quickly gave her an outline of the situation. They did not have time to give all the details but Jess was excited that Daniel might not have fallen into the sea. Like Granny, she felt sure he could not have survived a night in the sea or on a beach.

'Buried bones!' said Jess. 'Things are getting complicated. Well, just remember, if you want anyone to help with a rescue mission, count me in. I'd like to get my teeth into Meanwhisker.'

As she spoke, the children saw that the Colonel had reached the counter and was alone in the shop with the sisters. Ingrid weighed out his customary bag of humbugs as the Colonel fumbled in his pocket for cash. Humbugs and money were exchanged. Then Astrid spoke and the Colonel paused, his hand in mid-air holding the bag. She had been standing at the other end of the counter but now approached the Colonel and handed him an envelope. She and Ingrid held a finger to their lips in a gesture of silent conspiracy. Then they smiled and nodded, smiled and nodded.

The Colonel stared at them both for a moment, said something, then turned and left the shop.

'Damned peculiar thing,' said the Colonel as he crossed the road to the waiting children. 'Envelope from Astrid. Addressed to you. Important, she said. About the Akram boy.'

He held out an oblong cream envelope.

'What's he saying?' asked Jess.

Tilly still had her hand on the Stone and Jess got the drift from her surprised response.

'An envelope? From Astrid? For us?' she stuttered. 'About Daniel?'

Olly grabbed the envelope. The contents felt quite bulky. On the outside it said: *Mr O. and Miss T. Peterson.* He tore it open. The paper inside was thick and slightly rough to the touch, creamy yellow with ragged edges. It looked old. The writing on it was in capitals.

'IF YOU WISH TO SEE DANIEL AKRAM AGAIN,' Olly read to himself, 'DELIVER THE STONE TO THE MISSES BOYLE BY NOON TODAY.'

'Well, what does it say?' asked Tilly impatiently. Olly handed her the note.

'What does it say?' asked Jess impatiently. 'What have those Boyles done to Daniel? I think I'll go and bite them while I'm waiting.' She trotted off but the Colonel called her back. He craned his neck, trying to see the note.

Tilly was still holding the Stone.

This is awful, she thought.

Yes it is, thought Olly in reply.

Their eyes met in astonishment. This was new. They received each other's thought even though only Tilly was holding the Stone. There was no time to discuss it.

We need to get this note to Section H.Q. right away, she said.

Yes.

We still don't know if we can trust the Colonel, she went on.

His delivering the message makes me more suspicious. On the other hand, he did look really surprised when he came out of the shop just now. I don't know whether to show it to him or not. She paused for a fraction of a second, not sure what to do.

We mustn't take any risks, Olly sent. *Only one thing to do. Run for it.*

'Come on, Jess,' Tilly shouted and the two children sprinted off downhill. The dog, always game for action, leapt joyfully after them.

The Colonel was taken by surprise. The communication between the children had taken no more than two seconds, so it seemed to him that they had run off immediately after reading the note. By the time he recovered himself, there was no hope of catching them up.

'Curse it,' he muttered. He badly needed information from the children and he wished he had been able to read the note. Still, he knew a lot more than he did a few days ago.

He turned to look into the shop window. The two sisters were looking out. Smiling and nodding, smiling and nodding.

***

Out of breath from running, the children arrived at the entrance to Section H.Q. with Jess at their heels. She could easily have overtaken them but since she did not know where they were going she had to keep behind. She pranced and frolicked to show that she could have gone faster.

It was just before 9 o'clock. A mouse had been stationed to keep watch for them to let them in. There were a few other people about and the mouse signalled the children to wait until they had passed. Olly looked down towards the Dock and saw Mr and Mrs Akram coming out of their front door with Kiran. They looked pale and drawn. Mrs Akram dabbed her eyes with a handkerchief.

'Wait here,' said Olly and ran down to see them.

'We're off to search,' he lied. 'Can Kiran come with us?' Olly looked hard at Kiran and waggled his left ear, an old trick of his, to indicate that it was important.

'If she wants,' said Mr Akram. 'We are just going up to the Mobile Incident Room to wait for news but I can understand if she wants to do more than wait.' He looked miserable.

Kiran opted to go with Olly.

18

DECISIONS

'We've a lot to tell you,' said Olly as they hurried back up to the Section H.Q. entrance.

'Er, don't look now but there's a mouse waving at us,' said Kiran, astonished.

'Beckoning actually,' said Tilly. 'Come on.'

There was no one else around now and the entrance was opening.

Kiran gaped.

'I wasn't told anything about a dog, or a third human,' said the mouse doubtfully as they all trooped down the steps.

'They're with us,' said Olly, 'it's alright.'

'What *is* going on?' demanded Kiran. For the second time that morning Olly and Tilly explained. Kiran wept with relief and hope as she heard that Daniel might be alive after all.

Passing the door to the sick bay, the children were shown into a conference room with a large oval table. In the middle of one side of the table sat Aristotle Badger, with Wickfeather perching on the chair to his right. Liam sat on Aristotle's left with several other members of the section and Dauntless Arvicola beyond. Next to him was a sleek mole in a maroon beret and military uniform with a lot of gold braid on his shoulder, who Wickfeather introduced as the Mole-Major, Leader of the Mole Commandos.

Their old friend Heron, preening himself at one end of the table, looked up and greeted them. Tilly introduced Kiran and everyone commiserated about

Daniel. She also introduced Jess who eyed the birds suspiciously.

Dauntless Arvicola's nose flashed red and purple with alarm at Jess's size but he concealed his feelings as best he could by intently studying some papers on the table in front of him.

The mice were on a high mahogany bench with a ladder at either end. This was also suitable for the Mole-Major, not being that much bigger than a mouse. Dauntless Arvicola was somewhat bigger and had a separate stool. Aristotle, of course, had his own chair.

Olly and Tilly sat next to each other touching the Stone, and Kiran, next to Tilly, touched it too. Jess sat beside Olly on a chair, a rare treat, with a paw on his arm.

'We have some important news,' said Tilly to Aristotle, handing him the envelope.

At that moment the door opened and a rather pale Ian walked in, supported on the arm of a smiling Nurse Elaine. A ripple of applause went round the room, for news of last night's events had reached everyone. Ian took a place at the table with Nurse Elaine beside him.

Everyone watched Aristotle withdraw the parchment from the envelope and unfold it. Adjusting the glasses on his nose, he stared hard at the message, brow furrowed.

After a moment, he read it out and there was a stunned silence.

'Well,' Aristotle continued, 'let us examine this message. First, it fully confirms Ian's report that Daniel Akram did not fall into the sea. That's certainly good as far as it goes but it doesn't mean that Daniel is safe. Second, it threatens us with the loss of the Stone which we believe is needed to awaken Odric Scar. So, friends, we must decide what to do. You will all have a chance to speak.'

Dauntless Arvicola's nose flashed red with alarm at the thought of addressing the meeting. Liam gave him a reassuring smile.

Aristotle looked at his watch.

'We have less than three hours. After thirteen hundred years it is precious little time. Wickfeather, you speak first.'

'We are faced with a stark choice,' said Wickfeather, speaking in Rabbit as Aristotle had done. 'To prevent further harm coming to Daniel, we must hand over the Stone which will presumably be passed to Botwulf who will wake Odric, probably underground. Yet that will lead to dire consequences for the country and us all. If we do not hand it over, we avoid those consequences but such a course would surely mean the end of Daniel. In my view neither course is acceptable.'

A murmur of assent went round the table.

'Yes but we've got to do something.' Liam protested. 'We can't just drop into the Boyles' shop and say, 'Sorry, we're not playing your game so return Daniel to us and can I have a quarter of liquorice allsorts please.' Several mice tittered.

Ian agreed. 'He's right. We have to find a way that stops Botwulf getting the Stone and keeps Daniel alive.'

'Now you're starting to talk my language,' put in Jess. 'How about grabbing the two Boyles and their pesky cat and shaking them with our teeth until they tell us where Daniel is and how we can get him back.'

Heron, who had been preening and listening at the same time, snorted.

'Typical of a dog to approach the problem like a bull in a china shop,' he said scornfully. 'Hasn't it occurred to you, my furry friend, that it only takes one bat to tell Botwulf, and Daniel's had it.'

Jess was furious.

'At least it's doing something. Just sitting there poking your beak up your bottom won't get us anywhere.'

'I'm not poking my beak up my bottom,' said Heron angrily. 'Don't start…'

'Friends, friends,' Aristotle interrupted tactfully, 'let us not argue among ourselves. We are all upset by the present circumstances which perhaps makes us more touchy than would otherwise be the case. We must try to show restraint and to respect each other's point of view. I agree with Jess…'

Heron almost snorted again and Jess looked pleased.

'…It would indeed be sweet to strike a blow at the enemy but I also agree with Heron…'

Heron's neck went swan shaped and Jess growled quietly.

'…There are too many unknowns at this stage to be confident of success. There will, I am sure, come a time for a frontal assault but I feel it is not quite yet. Does anyone have any other suggestions?'

Olly stroked Jess's ears with his free hand to help calm her down.

One of the enthusiastic younger mice sitting between Liam and Dauntless Arvicola spoke up. His name was Jack.

'Couldn't we sort of pretend to hand over the Stone but hand over something else which looks like it but is really a bomb that explodes when it gets to Botwulf?'

Heron snorted again.

'Good thought, Jack,' said Liam quickly, anxious to head off another confrontation, 'but technically very difficult. For instance, how could we be sure that it wouldn't explode when Daniel was around. We don't want to blow him up by accident.'

'Oh yes,' said Jack giggling with embarrassment, 'I hadn't thought of that.'

'What if they've done something horrible to Daniel?' said Tilly looking anxiously at Kiran

'W-well we don't have to hand over the Stone unless we have p-proof that D-daniel is alright,' said Dauntless Arvicola. He had been listening intently and taking notes.

There was a short silence. He had surprised everyone with his insight. Liam looked at him in admiration.

'S-so we have a sort of exchange,' he went on. 'B-but then what?' His nose flashed bright red. His command of Rabbit was only just up to saying what he had said.

'The Captain has, I believe, accurately summed up the debate so far,' said Aristotle. 'We offer to deliver the Stone in return for Daniel but we do not have to stop there, as the Captain so succinctly implied.'

Dauntless Arvicola's Rabbit was not quite good enough for him to understand 'succinctly implied' and his nose turned rose pink as he busied himself writing to cover his confusion.

'What if the Boyles refuse to make the exchange?' asked Tilly.

'It could mean Daniel's not alive,' said Kiran, swallowing a sob.

'If they r-refuse an exchange we could h-hand over the S-Stone but f-follow them or something and try to get it b-back and rescue D-daniel at the same t-time.'

'Good idea!' Liam exclaimed. 'Then we've given them no excuse to dispose of Daniel and there's a chance for him.'

Aristotle, looked round the table.

'Right. We seem to have reached decisions. Olly and Tilly propose an exchange to the Boyle sisters. If they agree, well and good. We get Daniel then try to retrieve the Stone. If they don't agree, we hand it over and still try to get it back but we also mount a rescue mission for Daniel.'

'Yes,' shouted Jess a little too loudly, pleased to hear someone proposing action at last. This time her view was echoed by everyone even Heron. Olly ruffled Jess's neck fur affectionately.

The Mole-Major spoke for the first time.

'My commandos and I will be happy to help liberate Daniel or the Stone or both, especially if it involves underground assault as I strongly suspect it will. May I suggest that whether or not Daniel is released in exchange for the Stone one or two of the larger species among us follows the Stone and sends a message of its location when it looks as though it has come to rest?'

That sounds like us, thought Olly to his sister. Just as they were about to say so, Kiran and Jess spoke.

'I volunteer,' they said simultaneously.

'Us, too,' said Olly. Tilly nodded.

'You'll need mice, though,' said Liam. 'For technical support and to get into small places. How about me and Jack?'

Jack looked pleased.

Aristotle smiled for the first time. It lifted his spirits to see such enthusiasm in the face of danger.

'Our way forward is clear then,' he said. 'Whatever the outcome of Olly and Tilly proposing an exchange to the Boyles, we'll need a group that's ready secretly to follow the Stone, if necessary down the tunnels. It will be the three children with Liam, Jack and Jess. The Commandos will stand ready for a raid either to retrieve the Stone or rescue Daniel or both'

It was also agreed that Wickfeather and Heron would patrol the entire district from the air and Dauntless Arvicola would patrol the coast in the *SS Dauntless*.

'I think we can adjourn the meeting for the moment,' said Aristotle. 'I suggest the Stone followers get together to make plans and we reconvene for a final briefing in about an hour's time, say eleven o'clock,'

The Stone followers decided to base themselves in Daniel's bedroom ready to go wherever the Stone went.

'We've got just over half an hour to get some stuff together,' said Olly. 'We'll pack it in my rucksack and take turns to carry it.'

'I'll get some food,' said Kiran. 'Mum's always got lots of leftovers in the fridge. I'll go for it now and dump it under Daniel's bed.'

With that, the three children rushed off. Liam and Jack, with help from Ian, packed some equipment and emergency rations.

'This cheese is that new low odour stuff,' said Liam, nibbling a bit. 'Tastes like mature Lancashire but a cat can't smell it unless it's right under its nose.'

19

EXCHANGE

Shall we leave a note for Grandpa?

In a remarkably short time the children had adapted to telepathy when they were both touching the Stone but today it was happening when only one of them was.

Maybe we're getting better at it. Olly was holding it and they were in their room back at the cottage getting the rucksack. Grandpa would be up at the Village Hall.

They thought carefully. How could they cram all the information into a few lines, which is all they had time for? Also Granny might see it.

We'll phone him.

Olly dialled his number – and after a moment they heard a mobile ringing downstairs.

Typical.

They were not really surprised. Grandpa hardly ever carried his phone with him and even if he did, more often than not it was switched off. Granny didn't even have one.

We promised to tell him what's going on but we haven't time to go up to the Village Hall and explain.

Maybe we could use the Stone, said Olly suddenly. *Grandpa's descended from Alfred just like us so it might work.*

They decided to try together to give it more strength and sat at the table touching the Stone with their eyes closed.

Grandpa, can you hear us?

At that precise moment Grandpa was in the village hall lifting a heavy tea urn onto a trestle table under the supervision of Granny and Mrs Hutton. It was tall, cylindrical and shiny so he had to clasp his arms round it in front of him, making it difficult to see where he was going. He puffed and panted, getting a bit sweaty with the effort. He half-heard voices and felt irritated that anyone, presumably Granny and Mrs Hutton, expected him to hold a conversation while carrying the urn, so he ignored them until he had carefully lowered it into position.

'What did you say, dear?' he said, out of breath.

The children heard and smiled.

'Nothing to you Bill' replied Granny. She carried on gossiping to Mrs Hutton.

It was us, Grandpa. Please listen carefully.

There were two voices, he thought. It sounded like the children but a bit faint.

'I hear you,' he said, looking round, 'but where are you?'

His wife was too busy to notice.

Grandpa, please listen and don't say anything. We're at the cottage, sending thoughts to you by the power of the Stone.

They quickly outlined the situation to him.

We really don't know what's going to happen so if we don't come home tonight please cover for us if you can. We're sorry but we must go now, we have very little time. Is all that OK?'

Yes. Grandpa was gradually grasping what was happening and that he did not need to speak. *Anything else I can do?*

No thanks, except don't tell anyone about it, even the Colonel.

Good luck then and take care of yourselves.

The children broke the connection.

In the village hall Grandpa turned pale as the significance of the children's message sank in. He staggered back against the trestle table, and the urn almost toppled over.

'Are you alright, Bill?' asked his wife.

'Just a little dizzy, dear,' he replied, sitting down on a nearby chair. 'The tea urn was heavier than I expected.'

***

The reconvened meeting at Section H.Q. did not take long. Olly outlined the Stone followers' plan and Liam reported that communications were organised.

'Mobiles won't work underground unless there are repeaters, which there aren't, so we're using geophones.'

Everyone looked blank except Jack who nodded and Ian who said: 'Good idea.'

Dauntless Arvicola said his ship would put to sea at noon, fuelled and provisioned for at least a week. Everyone said they hoped Daniel would be free and the whole business resolved in a much shorter time than that but apparently Dauntless Arvicola's father and grandfather had always said, 'B-better safe than sorry.'

'When you and Tilly go to see the Boyles, you'd better leave the rucksack with me,' said Kiran to Olly. 'We don't want them guessing you're on a mission.'

After the meeting broke up, Aristotle and Wickfeather took Olly and Tilly on one side.

'Two more things,' said Aristotle. 'Firstly, our librarians have worked out that the thirteen hundred years since Odric became captive expire at midnight tonight. Secondly, despite the serious consequences of losing control of the Stone, you must not unnecessarily put yourselves at risk. Your power to use the Stone is unique and if your mission fails on this occasion, it is important that you survive to fight another day.'

Wickfeather agreed.

Not for the first time that day the children felt a pang of fear and a sense of the dangers they might face. They could not think of anything to say so they just nodded and there was a short silence.

'Well, it remains only to wish you Good Luck,' said Aristotle, smiling solemnly. Wickfeather dipped his beak twice.

It was ten to twelve. Olly and Tilly arranged to meet Kiran, Liam and Jack in Daniel's bedroom as soon as they could and hurried off to the Boyles' shop.

'Welcome, chidldrennn,' said Astrid, the hair on her nose wart wafting in the breeze from the open shop door. There were no customers in the shop and both sisters were behind the counter. Meanwhisker, curled up on a shelf, opened an eye.

'Welcome chidldrennn,' said Ingrid, her lazy eye rolling. The children did not feel like exchanging pleasantries.

'You want the Stone, well here it is.' said Tilly, holding it out.

The two sisters leaned forward eagerly.

'We're prepared to give it to you but only in exchange for Daniel,' said Olly.

'Exchange?' the sisters hissed at each other. There was no surprise in their tone – but something else that the children could not identify. Relief? Triumph? They had no time to dwell on it.

'Yes, *exchange*,' said Tilly. 'You produce Daniel and we hand over the Stone.

'Agreeed,' said Astrid. The pitch of her voice started high and fell to the end of the word.

'Agreeed,' echoed Ingrid.

The two children were surprised but pleased.

'OK then, where is he?' asked Olly.

'Downnnn,' said Astrid.

'Tunnelllsss,' said Ingrid.

'When can you produce him?'

'Now - if you come downnn with us,' they said together, smiling and nodding first at the children, then at each other. 'Longgg way downnn.'

'You mean we have to go down into the tunnels to get him?' asked Tilly. 'Why can't you bring him here?'

'Can't,' said Astrid.

'Can't,' said Ingrid.

'But why?' Tilly persisted.

'Can't,' they both repeated. '*He* says so.'

Olly was thoughtful. 'Just a minute, please. I want to talk to my sister.'

He pulled Tilly out of the shop and walked a little distance up the hill so the Boyle sisters could not see or hear them.

This is something we hadn't really expected but I think we have to say yes.

Tilly started to protest but he cut her short.

Think about it. If we agree, we find Daniel straightaway. Of course it could be a trick but we can hang onto the Stone until we see him. I'm saying 'we' but just in case it goes wrong I think only one of us should go – me.

Tilly started to protest again but Olly continued.

Look, I'm bigger and stronger than you so I'll be able to deal with any trouble better than you. You and Kiran should still follow with the mice and Jess. I'll send you messages using the Stone.

Tilly did not like the idea but could see the advantage of keeping control of the Stone until they found Daniel. She really wanted to go back and discuss it with the others but there was no time. She tried not to think about the darkness and the danger of the tunnels that Olly would be facing – on his own if she did not go with him. Oh, what should she do, she wailed to herself in her mind. She clutched the Stone tightly in a turmoil of indecision.

Suddenly, clarity came to her. Olly was right. Aristotle had said their power was unique. They should not take unnecessary risks. Both of them going with the sisters would be like putting all their eggs in one basket.

You're right, said Olly.

She had been so caught up in her thoughts she had forgotten he could receive them. She handed him the Stone as though to confirm their decision. They went back into the shop.

'I'll come with the Stone but not Tilly,' said Olly. The sisters did not argue.

Tilly wanted to say all sorts of things to her brother about being careful and keeping himself safe but all she could think of was a lame 'See you later.'

With that she turned and walked out of the shop.

Don't worry, I'll be alright, Olly sent.

20

CURWALD

After Botwulf had pulled the lever that dropped Daniel into the pit, he had handed the sisters the envelope. He had also told them to expect an exchange to be proposed and had authorised them to accept, even though he had no intention of handing Daniel over. As they left, he was looking forward to hearing Curwald tear Daniel limb from limb. It would happen very soon.

Then a thought struck his evil mind. Alfred's descendants might well have discovered some of the powers of the Stone. It might not be straightforward to take it from them. He needed something extra – some bargaining power that would enable him to apply pressure.

His unnaturally sharp hearing detected a snarl of triumph from Curwald and a long shout of shock and fear from Daniel. Botwulf made a decision. He hurried across the chamber and pulled the second lever.

An iron grill thudded down into a gap of four centimetres between Curwald's open jaws and Daniel's head. As Daniel tried to jump clear it trapped the rope trailing from his neck and pinned it to the ground. He knelt to free it if he could.

Botwulf's face twisted into a smile. Curwald would not understand why his meal had to be postponed but the boy might be useful when it came to negotiating the handover of the Stone.

Curwald roared, furious. Being denied his kill put him into an angry blood-lust. He was hungry. He longed for the exhilaration of fangs penetrating heart, of blood pumping into his mouth and onto his tongue. Why did his master torment him like this?

Then Curwald saw an opportunity. He pushed a paw through the bars, snagged the rope and pulled. Daniel struggled desperately but was dragged towards the ironwork until his back was hard up against it. He felt claws on his shoulder, ripping first clothes then flesh. He was so frightened he felt no pain. A rough and pitted tongue supped fresh blood from the wounds. It slithered up to his head to lick the now congealed blood from cuts caused by his earlier fall.

The noose was so tight round Daniel's neck he could hardly breathe and the more he struggled the more it compressed his windpipe. He gasped for breath, but none came and still the rope pulled tighter as Curwald tried to haul his meal through the bars. Daniel's mouth opened and shut like a fish out of water but no air passed. His eyes bulged and he thought his chest would burst.

As he lost consciousness he thought longingly of home.

A moment later Botwulf emerged from a concealed door. Daniel was limp and blue in the face, his tongue hanging out. Botwulf quickly removed the noose from his neck and slapped Daniel's face to wake him up.

'Back, Curwald, back,' he commanded. 'Have patience. You will be fed soon enough.'

The beast snarled angrily but retreated.

As Daniel came round, the pain hit him. He gasped and convulsed. The shredded flesh on his shoulder would have been agony even if he was lying still. As it was, every breath, every muscle movement was excruciating. On top of that his head ached, his mouth was dry and his tongue was swollen. He groaned and even that hurt.

Gradually, however, he regained control of himself and was able to lie quietly on the cold rock floor. Botwulf swam into his vision, smell preceding him. A small lantern cast a dim light.

'Get up, boy,' he grated.

Daniel tried to sit up but the pain from his shoulder was too great and he flopped down again.

'Get up I say, or shall I put one of your feet through the bars?'

Daniel was almost past caring but had just enough wit left to know that Botwulf would probably do as he threatened, so he tried again. This time he remained sitting up but cried out as his wounds stretched. He looked round and for the first time could see Curwald properly. A giant wolf with pointed ears, red eyes, shaggy grey hair and jaws that would crush a football as easily as an egg. He would have shuddered if it was not such torture.

'Come, boy, stand,' said Botwulf impatiently.

Slowly and painfully Daniel got to his feet. Botwulf pointed to the door and prodded him to walk in front. Through it there was a long tunnel with a spiral staircase at the end. At the top was a door into Botwulf's room. Once there Daniel sank to his knees, hurting everywhere, semi-conscious.

'You may wait here, boy,' said Botwulf. The harsh-edged voice jarred on Daniel's ears.

Wait for what, he wondered. I've had enough surprises for one day but it sounds as though there's more to come.

Escape did not enter his mind. He hardly knew if he was alive or dead. In the weak light he saw a black rug beside the wall, threadbare in places. He collapsed onto it and fell unconscious.

***

As Liam left for Daniel's bedroom, Ian caught him at the Section H.Q. entrance.

'Take this with you,' he said. 'You lost yours yesterday.' He handed Liam a pearl-handled catpin. Liam knew it had been in Ian's family for generations.

'I couldn't possibly,' he said, embarrassed. 'It's too valuable.'

'Well just take care of it then,' said Ian, smiling. 'And yourself.'

***

Bill Peterson was thoughtful as he sat in the village hall, to outward appearances recovering from a dizzy spell.

'You've only yourself to blame,' scolded Granny. 'You go at it too quickly. Take things more gently. Remember you're not as young as you were.'

She and Mrs Hutton nodded to each other.

He wondered mildly how you could take things gently whilst lifting a heavy weight like the tea urn but he said nothing. He knew it was something else that was affecting him. The children were going into great danger, he was quite sure. He wondered if he should have told them not to go or insisted on going along to protect them but it was too late now. Or maybe he could still get some help. He would speak to the Colonel, despite what the children had said.

'I'm just going out for some fresh air, dear,' he said. 'I'll see you later.'

Granny hardly looked up from her conversation. He did not know where she and Mrs Hutton found all the gossip they exchanged but they seemed to have an endless supply. The hall was now getting quite busy as searchers queued for food. The two women continued talking as they served.

Outside it was still cold and windy with squally showers. Bill Peterson put on his hat and headed down towards the Colonel's shop.

The Colonel was just arriving back, damp and windswept. He carried a plastic bag from the bakery.

'Searched all morning,' he said. 'Nothing. Seen the children? Odd thing. Ran off. Took Jess.'

'A lot of odd things seem to have happened since our last talk,' said Bill Peterson. 'Have you time for another short chat?'

'Delighted.' said the Colonel. 'Join me?' He held up the bag, which contained two sandwiches. They went inside and sat down to share them in the Colonel's living room.

'Tea?' asked the Colonel, jumping up to fill the kettle. 'Just check for emails,' he added, striding over to the computer. There was one waiting.

'Look,' he said bending over the keyboard to decrypt a message.

Bill Peterson looked at the screen and his heart sank as he read. It told of Olly taking the Stone down the tunnels with the Boyles and of Tilly about to follow with others. The signature was 'A. Regdab.'

'Who's that?' he asked.

'Long story,' said the Colonel. 'Tell you when there's time. To do with our talk last week.'

'I've followed your wishes and kept what you said to myself,' said Bill Peterson, 'but now I'm so worried about the children. I never thought their involvement would go this far.'

The Colonel shook his head sympathetically. He knew it could go a lot further.

21

DOWN

From the Boyles' shop Tilly headed straight for the Akrams as arranged.

'Where's Olly?' asked Kiran as she let her in the front door, with Jess fussing around. Tilly explained.

'Do you think he'll be alright?' Kiran asked.

'I just don't know,' said Tilly, her lip trembling. 'He said he would but he couldn't really say anything else could he?'

The front-door letter box, near ground level, opened a crack as Liam and Jack climbed in. They both carried small rucksacks. Jess bounded up and gave them a lick-greeting. Jack fell over.

Liam straightened his glasses and smiled, gesturing to be picked up. Tilly held him at eye level and saw that he carried a mouse-sized tablet. He was speaking into it then held it out. She squinted at the tiny screen, just able to make out a message scrolling across it.

'A, W know O + stne with Boils,' it said. She smiled at the spelling and assumed A and W meant Aristotle and Wickfeather. She was glad that mice are good at English and pleased that the news had travelled so fast. I should have realised they'd be listening, she thought.

'Good, but how are we going to know when Olly and the Boyles set off?'

Liam pointed to Jack who was hurrying upstairs towards Daniel's bedroom. They all followed and watched as Jack took off his rucksack to squeeze under the skirting board in one corner. In a moment he reappeared, pulling one end of a wire. He attached it to a small telephone handset from his bag and sat down to wait.

'Line to Section H.Q.?' Kiran asked.

Liam nodded.

'By the way,' she added, 'can you tell Jess what's happened?' Liam used Rabbit to bring Jess up to date.

Jess, like the rest of them, was worried about Olly being on his own. 'I could have gone with him,' she said to Liam. 'Then if the sisters tried anything clever, I could bite their feet off.'

While they were waiting, Tilly and Kiran packed food and some water into the rucksack. Olly's torch was already in there along with a small first aid kit. Olly had been wearing a waterproof jacket so he would probably be warm enough – the children thought it could be cold in the tunnels – but he had no food or other equipment.

Tilly looked longingly at some chocolate poking out of the top of the rucksack.

'No you don't,' said Kiran forcefully. 'That's all for later but I brought something else for now.' From under Daniel's bed she produced two spoons and a dish from the fridge with some of Mrs Akram's legendary rice pudding from the previous night.

Liam sat on the bed gnawing a small piece of cheese and watching Jack intently. Suddenly, Jack raised a front paw as though to call for quiet. Liam stood up and the girls stopped eating. Jack said something into the handset and turned towards them giving a thumbs-up sign.

Liam spoke to his tablet. 'O etc in tunl. Pass here 2 min. We go in 4?'

'Fine,' said the girls.

He repeated the plan to Jess, while Jack disconnected the wire.

'Well, we're on our own now,' he said.

Kiran spotted a small torch on the floor near Daniel's

bed. She put it in her pocket after checking that it worked.

After four minutes, Tilly and Kiran pulled one side of the bookcase to open the door. They had not tried it before and were working only from Ian's report of the previous evening. It would not budge.

'Try the other side,' suggested Tilly. This time they felt a small movement.

'Pull harder,' said Kiran.

The door swung open and they felt damp, cold air.

'Remember – from now on, absolute quiet,' Kiran whispered. 'Once the door's open, anyone down in the tunnel might be able to hear us.' Liam translated to Jess.

Tilly shouldered the rucksack and put Liam in her coat pocket. Jack bedded down comfortably in Kiran's jacket pocket among the kite and string, still there from the previous weekend. Treading softly, with Jess following, the girls started down the stone staircase, pausing only to pull the door shut behind them.

At the bottom the tunnel sloped down to the left and up to the right. They paused to listen but heard nothing.

'Let's go,' whispered Kiran. 'We don't want them to get too far ahead. And let's see if we can manage without torches. Remember even Ian's little torch gave him away.'

The others nodded.

'It's better if you look out of the sides of your eyes,' whispered Tilly. 'They're more sensitive than the middle. I saw it on telly.'

But it was total darkness and they kept stumbling which made too much noise. So Tilly got Olly's torch out and pointed it backwards with a glove over it, which gave just enough light in front of them but very little risk of the Boyles seeing it.

Tilly hoped to receive some thoughts from Olly soon.

They continued walking in silence for about an hour, taking turns to carry the rucksack and pausing every now and then to listen but never hearing anything. Nothing from Olly either. They passed several forks and always chose the downhill tunnel. What if they've gone a different way, thought Tilly.

Then suddenly: *We've stopped.* It was Olly, sounding quite near.

Instinctively Tilly almost shouted back but stopped herself in time.

At last! Where are you? As soon as she sent it she realised it was a silly question.

In the tunnel, where do you think? The Boyles have been mumbling about lunch for half an hour and they've finally decided to have some sandwiches.

'Olly's in touch,' Tilly whispered to Kiran. 'They've just stopped so we'd better stop too.'

The sandwiches look disgusting. There's hairy things sticking out at the sides like spider legs. I'm hungry myself but not enough to eat their horrible food.

Yuck. Let us know when you set off again.

OK. By the way tell Liam and Jack to be careful because Meanwhisker is with us.

Tilly relayed the news and Liam translated for Jess, who was pleased. 'I'd like to bump into Meanwhisker – very hard indeed.'

Liam nervously fingered the pearl-handled catpin. 'Don't joke about it.' he said.

'I'm not,' said Jess.

Right, we're off again, Olly sent after a while. *If you don't hear from me we're still moving.*

Olly and the Boyle sisters walked for another hour by the light of Astrid's weak torch.

Suddenly, a deep growling filled Olly's head. He tripped over a stone and almost went sprawling.

'Clummmsy,' said Ingrid, eye rolling.

'Clummmsy,' Astrid repeated.

Curwald's keen sense of smell had detected several meals walking past overhead.

The sisters had obviously not heard the growl, and Olly realised it must come through the Stone rather than his ears. It came from beneath their feet. He had an impression of a wild beast of some sort. It was very hungry and not happy. Like me, he thought.

Meanwhisker sensed danger, too, for she clung to Astrid's heels. There was also a smell of something rotten.

'Curwald.' The sisters tittered to each other, sniffing.

'Cur what?' asked Olly.

'Daniel's friennnd,' said the sisters one after the other, nodding vigorously. For all they knew, Curwald had already eaten Daniel.

Olly doubted if anyone could make friends with the beast he had heard. He sensed treachery.

'Is Daniel near then?' he asked innocently.

'Very, verrry near,' said Ingrid.

'Yesss, very verrry near,' said Astrid. The usual smiling and nodding. Then silence as they continued the journey.

Something strange here, Olly sent. *There's a bad smell and through the Stone I heard a beast growling under the tunnel floor. The sisters said its name and gave me some rubbish about it being Daniel's friend but they also say Daniel's near so we must be almost there now. Wherever there is.*

Less than two minutes later the girls smelled the smell.

'Phew,' said Jack to Liam, 'stinks worse than a cat's lavatory.' That was the worst smell a mouse could think of.

'I think we should stop,' said Tilly quietly. 'We must

have been closer behind them than we thought. We'll just let the gap open up a bit.'

'Well, not just here,' said Kiran. 'Let's get past this smell.' So they moved on a bit and sat down, leaning against the tunnel wall.

***

Botwulf's sharp ears heard the sisters and Olly approaching. His mind had also faintly detected something else. Communication using the Stone. He was excited to have proof that it was approaching yet concerned at the implications of what he heard. It was garbled, not like it had been centuries before. He could not tell who was using it or what was being said. The Stone must have been tampered with.

'Alfred, no doubt,' he muttered. 'No matter, I will repair it.'

The sisters and Olly turned off the tunnel into the passage leading to Botwulf's room and, passing the steps going down to the left, stopped at the door ahead.

Astrid knocked and pushed it open. Botwulf's eyes glittered in triumph as he saw Olly with them. How delighted his master would be, when he became conscious, to see a son of Alfred. How delicious would be his master's revenge.

'Come in…friends,' he croaked in a mocking tone. Olly winced at the voice. He found it every bit as jarring as Daniel had done.

Outwardly Botwulf's appearance was much as Olly expected. He had not been warned about the smell, though. Also there was something very cold and calculating about him.

'You have the Stone,' said Botwulf eagerly. It was a statement rather than a question and not addressed to any one of the three in particular.

'*He* has it,' said Ingrid, her sister echoing. They smiled and nodded, self-satisfied. They felt they had done well. They should be rewarded.

'Well then, hand it over,' spat Botwulf impatiently.

'Only when you hand Daniel over,' Olly spoke firmly, though he could feel himself trembling.

Botwulf snorted. Daniel, indeed! Why did people worry about each other so much. It was irritating and wasteful. Nevertheless, he told himself, he had anticipated it. His plan was foolproof. He must give the illusion of agreeing to an exchange in order to be reunited with the Stone. He had waited a long time. A little longer was nothing.

He was about to reply to Olly when his ears picked up a faint sound from the tunnel. Somewhere near the pit, he guessed. So the sisters and the boy had been followed. He had suspected it when he detected the Stone being used. How futile.

'Ah, yes,' said Botwulf trying to sound ingratiating but succeeding only in putting Olly's teeth on edge, 'you must see Daniel. Here he is.'

He walked to the back of the room and stood beside the levers, pointing to the black rug. As Olly rushed over to Daniel, Botwulf pulled one lever down and the other up. If Curwald was lucky, he might get a meal but if not, at least the tunnel was now impassable. And it must remain so, he thought, so that no-one from above can interfere with the plan. He turned a key beside one of the levers, locking it in position, then put the key into the folds of his cloak.

***

'Come on,' Kiran whispered, standing up, 'let's get closer to Olly.' She began to move quietly along the tunnel. 'Your turn to carry the rucksack.'

Tilly put it on and took a step back as she felt its full weight – but the ground had disappeared behind her. She yelped with fright. She was balancing on one foot, the other in empty space – and the rucksack was pulling her backwards. Waving her arms, she flung herself forward and sprawled full length on the ground, feet dangling over the edge. Liam leapt out of her pocket at the last minute to avoid being squashed beneath her.

In the pit Curwald roared his disappointment making Liam jump so much that his glasses, already askew after his emergency exit, fell off altogether.

Looking down, it was so dark they could see only Curwald's glowing eyes. Jess growled fiercely as Kiran shone her torch and revealed the full size and ferocity of the ancient beast.

Frightening though it was, they could see that it could not get out of the pit. Nonetheless they were alarmed at the thought of what might have happened.

'And it stops anyone getting in or out,' said Tilly dismally.

'I've never seen a wolf as big and weird as that,' said Liam after putting his glasses on again.

'When have you seen a wolf before?' asked Jack.

'Never, actually,' said Liam solemnly and they both giggled.

22

BARGAINING

In his room Botwulf heard Curwald but, unfortunately, no human screams or anything to suggest that anyone had fallen into the pit. Now all was quiet again.

Olly knelt beside Daniel. He seemed to be asleep or unconscious, lying on his left side. He had a deep cut and a large bruise on his forehead. The clothes on his back were torn from neck to waist and the flesh beneath was horribly gashed. Blood still seeped from the wounds and bone was exposed on his shoulders. He needed stitches and must have lost a lot of blood. Olly felt a great anger welling up inside him.

'What have you done to him?' he shouted at Botwulf.

'I?' rasped Botwulf contemptuously. 'I have done nothing to your friend. He brought it on himself.'

'Oh, very likely!' said Olly. His anger gave him courage and he stood up to face Botwulf.

'I'm afraid this means you don't get the Stone. At least not until Daniel's safely in hospital and the doctors say he's going to be alright.'

The Boyles bridled and tutted. The boy was being insolent. They had better show their disapproval or Botwulf might be displeased with them, too. For a moment, Botwulf's eyes flared in anger but he controlled himself. He had foreseen this. He must be calm.

'I think not,' he said evenly, ignoring the sisters and advancing towards Olly to overpower him.

'Stop there Botwulf,' shouted Olly, 'or I'll use the Stone to do something nasty to you.' He did not know if he could, or where his confidence was coming from but he felt the Stone in his pocket and it was comforting to touch.

Botwulf paused. He obviously believes me, thought Olly. This was partly true but also Botwulf had just heard more sounds from the tunnel. Whispering and light footsteps. The followers must have passed the pit before he opened it. Soon he might have additional hostages. Also, Botwulf needed to know how adept the boy was with the Stone and whether or not he could carry out his threat. He must play along for the moment.

'I have no wish to hurt you,' Botwulf lied, 'and perhaps before either of us does something we might regret, we need to discuss one or two things.'

'Like what?' asked Olly.

'Like how do I know the Stone you carry is the real Stone? I need you to demonstrate that it is not an imitation.' Botwulf tried to sound reasonable but his voice was not designed for it.

Poor Daniel, still unconscious, groaned loudly.

***

Kiran and Tilly saw the heavy door up ahead and paused.

What's happening? Tilly sent to Olly.

Daniel's here and alive but he's badly injured came the immediate reply.

Tilly told Kiran. The news both relieved and worried them.

What sort of injuries? asked Tilly.

His back's badly slashed. Looks as though he's been mauled by a lion or something with large claws.

Tilly could guess what had done it. She felt cold at the thought of Daniel in the wolf's clutches.

We'll come a bit nearer in case we're needed, she said. *Just be careful. By the way, you could try to help Daniel with the Stone.*

Olly could have kicked himself. He had been too busy

being angry with Botwulf to think of the obvious. They had been able to help Ian so why not Daniel?

As usual, the exchange between the two children had taken place in an instant. Botwulf was aware of it. Long disused parts of his brain tried unsuccessfully to decipher it. From the strength of the signal it was clear that the boy was at one end of the conversation and the other participant was near. It must be the daughter of Alfred. Better and better. If she, too, was a hostage, he could drive whatever bargain he liked and later tonight his master would be pleased. He listened carefully. Two humans and a four-legged creature of some sort.

Meanwhisker meandered towards Daniel, attracted by the smell of blood.

Don't you dare, Olly sent to Meanwhisker. She turned her head to look at him and hissed but kept away from Daniel.

'So you want proof this really is the Stone?' he said, holding it up.

Botwulf could not stop himself reaching for it. Olly snatched it away.

'Of course,' replied Botwulf expressionless. He already had proof, but needed to know the boy's ability to use it. Communication was nothing to fear but what else could he do? Also, the footsteps were much nearer now. He needed the boy to be distracted so that he did not send a warning.

'Let's start with something simple,' said Botwulf. 'See if you can frighten the cat.'

The sisters looked uncomfortable but dared not say anything.

'No,' said Olly. 'I'll see if I can use the Stone to help Daniel.'

Botwulf felt nothing but contempt for the boy's concern for his friend but he had learned something.

The boy believed he could and that went beyond mere communication.

Olly knelt down again. Daniel was still unconscious. His breathing had become irregular and he moaned every now and then. His forehead was very hot. Olly placed one hand on it and held the Stone with the other. He braced himself for the river feeling and closed his eyes.

Daniel, can you hear me, he said with his mind.

Nothing. No response. No contact.

Olly was dismayed. He had to help Daniel. What was he going to do? Try harder. He kept his eyes shut and concentrated.

Botwulf watched, a disdainful expression on his face, hoping the boy would fail, but not just yet. It would suit Botwulf if he kept his eyes shut a little longer. There were now faint sounds from the passage just outside the room. He left Olly and Daniel and edged quietly across towards the door, beckoning the sisters to follow.

Kiran, Tilly and Jess, with Liam and Jack still comfortably pocketed, had turned into the passage from the main tunnel and were almost there. The door was ajar and light shone out. They tiptoed forward to peek through.

They saw Olly kneeling beside Daniel. Olly's eyes were shut and he had one hand on Daniel's forehead. No one else was to be seen.

Tilly did not want to disturb her brother if he was helping Daniel but she wanted him to know they were there and could try to help. She tried a short message.

We're just outside the door, she sent.

Olly was startled. He opened his eyes.

Botwulf and the sisters were standing against the wall beside the door.

Get back he sent and shouted at the same time.

Too late.

Springing with unexpected agility through the doorway, Botwulf grabbed Tilly and the sisters grabbed Kiran.

Both girls struggled and kicked furiously. Jess barked loudly. She was as shocked as they were but excited as well – ready for a fight. Meanwhisker ran for cover.

Botwulf, much stronger than he looked, picked Tilly up and held her out in front of him so her feet could not touch the ground – or him. Jess did not know who to attack first but she saw Olly dart towards Tilly and Botwulf, so decided to go for the Boyles.

She clamped her jaws round Ingrid's ankle and pulled. Ingrid screeched in pain and let go of Kiran.

With her free fist Kiran thumped Astrid in the stomach. She was completely winded but did not release her grip. Instead she fell against Kiran, toppling the two of them to the floor.

Meanwhile Ingrid, eye rolling in pain, hopped around on one leg, Jess's jaws still tight around the other. Jess, snarling, was enjoying it apart from the bitter taste of Ingrid's blood.

As Kiran tried in vain to free herself, Jess decided to have a go at Astrid. She let go of Ingrid and bit Astrid's wrist. Again bitter blood and Astrid howled. But Ingrid, mad as a bee, recovered enough to land two vicious kicks in Jess's ribs, making the dog lose her grip. She was not badly hurt but the pain made her pause and pant for a moment and even in that short time the sisters managed to pin Kiran down.

Olly had thrown himself at Botwulf in a rugby tackle and knocked him to the floor, landing on top of his skinny legs. Botwulf fell heavily but still held Tilly in a tight grasp. She tried to squirm loose and managed to get one arm free. She rained blows on him but he seemed not to notice them and held fast to her other arm. It was like being gripped by a steel skeleton.

Olly was trying to hold on to Botwulf's now furiously kicking legs but he soon lost his grip. He and Botwulf sprang to their feet at the same time but before Olly had time to think Botwulf, still holding Tilly, ran at him sideways and shoulder-butted him in the chest. Olly staggered backwards, lost his balance and fell over, hitting his head on the stone floor. He saw bright lights for a moment then darkness.

Later he half came round as though in a dream. He was sitting down and looking at Tilly and Kiran but could not move his arms or his legs. They were saying something but he couldn't hear. His head rolled, blackness welling up again and as his eyes closed he saw Botwulf, one arm raised in front of him, holding the Stone.

23

LOCK-IN

Tilly and Kiran were crestfallen and frightened and also felt angry with themselves. Quite apart from being very worried about Daniel and Olly, they felt they had totally failed in their mission and let everyone down.

They saw no prospect of escape. They were each sitting in a straight-backed wooden arm chair, tied to it by their wrists, legs and chests. Olly was similarly tied to a chair facing them. The rucksack was on the floor near Kiran.

After Botwulf and the sisters had bound them all, Olly's eyes had opened for a moment or two and they tried to speak to him but he just looked vacant and dropped unconscious again. Jess, quiet now, sat beside him, her head resting on his feet, ready to attack anyone who came near.

Daniel looked really bad. His face was red and hot, his breathing was laboured and he groaned frequently. Obviously, whatever Olly had tried to do with the Stone had not worked.

When the fight with Botwulf and the sisters began, Liam and Jack had no option but to stay in their respective pockets and keep their heads down. They clung on for dear life and just had to hope they would not fall out or be squashed. It was a rocky ride but they came through it.

After things calmed down a bit they needed to have a look to see what had happened. They each remembered what their mothers had taught them and sprayed themselves with scent neutraliser. With Meanwhisker about they could not be too careful.

Tilly felt a movement in her pocket. Liam! She had forgotten about him in all the confusion. He might be able to do something to help. She looked across at Kiran and noticed a movement in her pocket. A tiny ear and one eye peeped out under its flap. Jack saw Tilly and winked. Tilly winked back then hastily swivelled her eyes round the room to make sure nobody was looking. It was alright. Botwulf was pacing around his table, gloating over the Stone and muttering to himself. The sisters had retreated to the back of the room to nurse their wounds. Meanwhisker had run off when Jess appeared and had not returned.

More movement from Liam. Whisker by whisker, his nose, his glasses then his whole head appeared from the pocket. He looked round cautiously. He had not been seen. He waved at Jack to stay down and turned to look up at Tilly. Quickly he scurried out of her pocket and round behind her arm. She felt him climb up her back near where it rested against the chair, then work his way under her coat collar. After a short pause, Liam thrust his tiny tablet out from under her lapel for a moment then drew it back. Tilly just had time to read it. It said: 'We call help.'

In an instant Tilly thought about it. Quite possibly Liam and Jack could gnaw through rope to release her or Kiran but Botwulf, the sisters or Meanwhisker would be bound to see. Going for help was a better idea – although she had no idea how they would do it.

'Ok,' she whispered, 'and thanks.'

'No talking.' croaked Botwulf, passing nearby.

Liam stayed where he was and the tablet appeared again: 'Jes too?'

A good idea, thought Tilly. Jess could protect the mice and it would keep her out of the way of the sisters, who might want revenge for their injuries. Tilly nodded discreetly.

Liam beckoned to Jack and pointed to Jess. Both mice, still with their rucksacks, worked their way to the floor using the cover of the chair legs.

Once on the ground they had to cross open floor to reach Jess but in the low light it was shadowy enough for them not to be noticed. When they reached Jess, they climbed up to hide comfortably under her silky ears.

In Rabbit, Liam quickly proposed that the three of them should go back up the tunnel a short distance and try to call for help using a geophone that Jack had in his rucksack.

Jess was worried about the children. They needed protection. She looked across at Tilly, who guessed what was going through the faithful dog's mind. Tilly nodded encouragingly as Liam told Jess that Tilly had said it was alright. So Jess quietly agreed.

Jess wore a leather collar that was quite broad and fairly loose fitting. Liam and Jack crawled underneath it at the back of Jess's neck and concealed themselves by fluffing up her soft hair.

Slowly, so as not to arouse suspicion, Jess stood up and stretched, first her front legs and then her back. She looked round for a moment then started to pad about the floor with her nose to the ground as though she was doing the normal doggy thing of following smells. Botwulf and the sisters took no notice.

Gradually, Jess widened the area of her operations until every now and then she passed the door, each time a little closer. Liam and Jack clung to her neck, their hearts in their mouths.

As Jess made one final pass by the chairs, she raised her head and ran for the door. She was just a few paces away from it when a shrill shout came from the shadows at the far end of the room. The sisters had seen her.

'The dog's gettinnng awayyyy,' Ingrid shouted.

They were too late. Jess was through the door, racing along the passage and out into the main tunnel.

Botwulf paused in his perambulations, stroking the Stone.

'No matter, sisters,' he said calmly, 'it is but a stupid lower animal and the tunnel is still impassable.' He gestured towards the levers at the back of the room.

So that was how the hole in the tunnel floor worked, thought Tilly. They had to get free to close it so that help could come down from the surface. Then help Daniel and Olly.

Olly groaned. He was rising up through layers of darkness, each one less black than the one before, then through shades of grey becoming lighter and lighter until finally there was whiteness and he could open his eyes.

His head thumped but he could feel his arms and legs and move them a little within their bindings. Seeing him stir, Tilly's spirits rose a little.

'Are you OK?' she asked out loud. Botwulf could lump it if he told her to be quiet.

'Yes,' he said trying his best to smile. 'My head hurts but everything else seems to be alright. Where's Jess?'

'She's just run off,' said Tilly, then silently mouthed, 'with Liam and Jack.' Olly raised his eyebrows.

'Sisters,' said Botwulf, ceasing his pacing, 'we have work to do in the laboratory. We must examine the Stone thoroughly and try some experiments. Come.'

They walked purposefully out of the door, their footsteps fading quickly as they turned right down the steps. So the laboratory was down there.

After a moment they heard a set of footsteps coming back and the door was slammed shut. A key turned in the lock and the footsteps retreated. They were locked in. They should have expected it but it worried them.

'Right,' said Tilly, 'there are scissors in the first aid kit in the rucksack. We must get out of these ropes.'

'If I topple my chair over,' said Kiran, 'I might just be able to reach the rucksack.'

Olly and Tilly measured it up with their eyes and agreed that it was possible.

Kiran rocked the chair from side to side so that first the left legs then the right left the floor, each time a little higher. Further and further the chair leaned at each rock. Suddenly there was a crack as one of the front legs gave way.

'Ow!' she shouted as the chair pitched sideways and a knee and elbow hit the ground. She was still tied to the chair but her right leg, the one on the ground, was now free with the broken chair leg attached like a splint. She had made a lot of noise so she lay still and they all listened. No sound from below.

She used her free leg to manoeuvre herself and the chair into a position where she could reach the rucksack with a hand even though her wrist was still tied to the chair arm.

'It's in the top flap, said Tilly. 'You need to unzip it.'

It took time but she was able to inch the zip open and pull out the first aid kit. It also had a zip but she soon had the scissors out. Reversing them in her hand she could use them to chew away at the rope around her wrist. The scissors were small but quite sharp so it would not take long.

Olly's head was starting to clear.

'You remember when you arrived,' he said, 'I was trying to use the Stone on Daniel?' Tilly nodded. 'Well it wasn't like when you and I helped Ian. I couldn't make any contact at all. I think it needs both of us to try together.'

'But now we haven't got the Stone,' said Tilly miserably. 'We'll just have to do what we can with the first aid kit.'

'Done it!' Kiran exclaimed. She had cut through the rope and her right hand was free. In a moment she was completely untied, apart from the splint on her right leg. Before starting on it she clopped over to Olly and Tilly to untie their hands so they could all be free in the shortest possible time.

As soon as they were, they hurried over to Daniel and gently turned him onto his front. Using sterile rubber gloves from the first aid kit, Olly carefully picked out dirt and shreds of clothing from the wounds on his back and gently smoothed antiseptic ointment into them. The first aid kit did not have enough dressings to cover all the wounds so he used what he had on the deepest. He also cleaned and put antiseptic in the cuts on Daniel's head.

Daniel groaned occasionally while Olly was at work. Kiran and Tilly stroked his head and although he was unconscious they told him quietly what Olly was doing. Kiran had read somewhere that people can sometimes still hear things when they are unconscious.

Daniel's forehead was burning and feverish but they had done all they could for now. The ointment might buy them some time.

They were not sure which of the two levers controlled the pit cover so they tried to move them both but one would not budge. Kiran found that by twisting the one that moved it could be unscrewed from its slot. It made a handy weapon, being oak or some similar wood, hardened with age.

Now they needed to get the Stone back.

24

BREAK-OUT

Jess kept on running as she passed through the rock door and turned up the tunnel, grinning broadly as she went. This was more like it. A bit of action. And she hoped the sisters' bites were still hurting.

Liam and Jack hung on tight to Jess's collar and shone their tiny torches to the front but they were jolted around so much that the beams flicked crazily about the tunnel walls and roof.

'Watch out for the pit!' shouted Liam, holding his glasses on with one hand as they hurtled round a bend.

Jess's emergency stop almost catapulted the mice over the top of her head but they just managed to hold on and avoid the dark void.

Curwald snarled miserably. He was depressed. No food yet despite the lovely smells that kept appearing overhead. On the positive side, things had not been so busy in the tunnel for centuries. Surely he would not have to wait long now. He salivated as he remembered the blood he had tasted earlier.

'Let's try the geophone,' said Jack, sliding down to the tunnel floor. Geophones were like telephones without wires but only worked when a long metal spike was hammered into the ground.

The two mice got it out of Liam's rucksack and walked around stamping their feet to find a soft place. They had a hammer but it would not drive the spike into rock. Eventually, Jack found a small patch where the floor was gravelly rather than solid rock. They took it in turns to hammer. It was hard going. After a while they managed to get about half the spike into the ground.

'Not far enough, really,' said Liam, shaking his head. 'To work properly it needs to be all the way in but I don't think it's going to go any further. Let's give it a try, anyway.'

Jack connected a wire from the spike to the phone unit, checked the batteries and flicked a switch. A red light came on.

He opened the lid of the unit, picked up a small telephone handset and adjusted some dials.

'Right, here goes,' he said, pressing the button on the handset. 'Hello H.Q. hello Ian, can you hear me? This is Liam.'

He heard nothing. He tried again. This time there was a faint reply, barely audible. Liam recognised Ian's voice.

'...lo Li... ..ow's ...ings.' The signal faded in and out.

'Daniel's alive but injured,' said Liam as loudly as he dared, lips pressed to the phone. 'Botwulf has the Stone. The children have been captured.'

'...ay again,' said Ian, '...ery weak...'

Liam tried again but Ian still could not get the message. The portable unit was much less powerful than the one at H.Q.

After a few more tries Liam gave up.

'It's no use,' he said, 'we need to find a better spot for the spike.'

'There isn't one,' said Jack dismally.

'I've been thinking,' said Jess. 'If I took a run, I bet I could jump over the pit.'

Without waiting for a reply, she trotted back a few paces, took a deep breath and ran at it.

Liam and Jack were horror-struck. What if she didn't make it?

The two mice gasped as they watched Jess race towards the edge and launch herself into the darkness.

There was a breathless pause – and they heard her land on the other side.

'Made it,' called Jess, laughing. 'See you later.' She turned and set off to the village. Down in the pit Curwald growled furiously.

'Cat's bottoms,' said Jack. 'I'm glad we got off Jess's back when we did.'

'Me too' said Liam. 'But what do we do now?

'Go back and help the children?' said Jack

'My thoughts exactly,' Liam replied.

***

The children thought they might be able to open the door. They slid one of the papers from Botwulf's table under it and tried to push the key out of the keyhole from the inside. In theory, it would land on the paper and they could pull it back into the room. It was not as easy as it sounded. The key was partially turned so it would not push out. Olly had just started poking into the keyhole with the scissors when they heard someone coming up the steps outside the door. They pulled the paper back and froze.

'Come, sisters,' they heard Botwulf say, 'we must prepare our master's chamber. The hour is fast approaching.'

Tilly peeped under the door and saw three pairs of feet walking away down the passage. Meanwhisker appeared and ran after them. Ingrid bent to pick her up.

'Hello, my little Queennn and where have you been hidinnng?' she said. 'Did that nasssty dog frighten you? Welll, we will have our revennnge. It will be painnnfulll and terrrminal.'

Both sisters sniggered as they repeated 'terrrminal' to each other, emphasising the first syllable.

Meanwhisker tried to interrupt to tell them she could

smell mouse but the sisters swept into the main tunnel, turning right after the hurrying Botwulf.

Fortunately, they failed to notice Liam and Jack pressed against the tunnel wall behind the heavy door.

'Crumbs,' said Liam, sweating, when they had passed. 'That was close.'

Cautiously, the mice peeped from the tunnel into the passageway. They could see the wooden door at the end.

'We'd better be very quiet,' Liam whispered, 'in case Meanwhisker comes back.'

As they tiptoed along the passage Tilly was still looking under the door.

'Liam!' she hissed urgently. 'Can you let us out?'

Jack looked up at the door key. It was a large iron one with an ornate ring. He took a length of string from his rucksack and, holding it in his teeth, climbed up the door. Tying one end to the bottom of key's ring he threw the other down to Liam who moved to one side and pulled.

Gradually the key straightened in the keyhole. Liam let go so Jack could pull the string up again and throw it over the door handle back down to the ground. Jack then sat on the key and pushed against the lock with his feet, gradually pulling it out while Liam held on to the string below. As the key came free Jack nimbly jumped clear and grabbed the edge of the keyhole. Liam gently lowered the key to the ground and quickly pushed it under the door.

'What now?' said Liam to his tablet, after the door was opened and children and mice had brought each other up to date. Jack was tucking into cheese.

'We must get the Stone to help Daniel,' said Olly. 'It's in the laboratory I think.'

Quietly, they left Botwulf's room and headed down the steps. Liam and Jack were back in the girls' pockets.

***

At Section H.Q. Ian and Aristotle had been together in the control room when Liam's geophone call came through. They were excited about it, but frustrated because they had not been able to make out what Liam was saying.

'I think Liam said something about Daniel,' said Ian, 'but I couldn't tell what. I can't understand it. The geophone's usually so reliable. Mind you, we've never used it so deep before, and if the tunnels are solid rock it may be difficult for them to hammer the spike in properly.'

Aristotle considered the position.

'I think we can assume,' he said, 'that the call was to tell us where the Stone is or to ask for help, or both.'

'We don't have much help to give, though,' said Ian. 'There's you, me, the rest of my mice and the Mole Commandos but we're all rather small. We could do with a few big clumsy humans to even up the odds a bit'

Mice generally regarded humans as big and clumsy but Ian had to admit that size had its uses.

Aristotle looked thoughtful.

'I think I'll brief the Mole-Major now,' he said. 'We don't know exactly where the children and the Stone are but it may be possible to make an educated guess using old plans from The First Book. In which case the Mole Commandos could go in right away.'

25

TRAP

The stone staircase was longer than the children expected, leading down to a cavern with a rock door on the other side, slightly ajar. Near the bottom of the steps was a square opening in the side wall and they poked their heads through. Their torches showed it was a shaft but they could not see the top or the bottom. There was an updraught that was warmer than tunnel air but it carried a fetid stench of decay.

'Yuck, I don't like the smell of whatever's down there,' said Olly. 'I wonder what it is.'

'I dread to think,' said Tilly.

They quickly withdrew from the shaft and headed towards the door.

'I wonder if there's an opening at the top though,' said Olly thoughtfully.

There was no time to investigate – they had to get the Stone to try to help Daniel. Through the rock door they found themselves in the laboratory.

It was large and quite well lit by Botwulf's standards. It needed to be, because it was absolutely full of equipment of all sorts, on tables, on chairs, on the floor, attached to the walls – everywhere. Test tubes, pipes and flasks bubbled. Lights flashed and control panels hummed.

All round the wall were cupboards, cabinets and drawers full of jars, bottles, wires, clips and many other unidentifiable items. It was difficult to move without banging into things.

Kiran, still carrying the lever, brushed against a table

and an empty flask fell off. Tilly, behind her, just caught it before it hit the ground.

Olly, Tilly and the mice looked at Kiran.

'What?' she said, sounding hurt. 'I didn't even touch it.'

Rather than risk accidents they tried to look round the lab from where they stood. Liam and Jack stepped out onto a table and climbed up a glass tube rising diagonally towards the ceiling.

'Look at that shiny wooden box with all those wires going into it,' said Liam to Jack. It was on a stand in the middle of the room. 'I bet the Stone's in there. I'll nip down and tell them.'

The others could not see it because it was hidden by a mass of scientific paraphernalia.

'You lot stay here,' said Olly after seeing the message on Liam's tablet. 'I'll take a look.' Liam went back up to Jack.

The box was the centrepiece of the laboratory. Its lid was open, and nestling in the black velvet interior was the Stone. Wires were taped to it, leading to flickering neon tubes and quivering meters. A pen moved up and down tracing a wiggly pattern on a chart recorder.

Liam was in technology heaven as he looked around from his lofty vantage point. Some equipment he recognised but the rest was new and intriguing. Even the ceiling was festooned with stuff, particularly near the Stone's box. Directly above it was a large circle of wire coils and, pointing downwards from the middle of it, a copper cone.

'If I'm not mistaken,' said Liam to Jack, 'that's a microwave transducer. But there's something odd about it. It looks as though the windings are fed in anti-phase.'

'Really?' said Jack vaguely.

'Yes,' said Liam getting excited, 'but what's more

extraordinary is that it's front-end modulated!'

'Oh,' said Jack, completely lost but not wanting to show it.

'And you know what that means don't you?' Liam babbled, not waiting for a reply. 'Instead of frying anything underneath, it fr…'

Suddenly his whiskers sat up like exclamation marks, the colour draining from his face.

Olly was reaching out for the Stone with both hands. He planned to pull the wires off it and remove it from the box.

'Stop,' shouted Liam as loudly as he could but of course in Mouse.

'What?' said Olly, not stopping.

A force from above, like a shimmering translucent curtain, suddenly gripped Olly's wrists. He could not move them. The force was cold. Deathly cold. His hands were instantly numb and there was frost on them. He felt cold creeping up his arms but he could not pull them away.

'Help,' he shouted.

Liam alone knew what had happened. Jack had only a hazy idea.

'I'm trapped and my arms are stuck and they're freezing.'

'Come on, Jack,' said Liam.

Olly was hidden from the others by the equipment in between.

'We're coming,' said Kiran, hurrying in his direction. Tilly caught *most* of the objects that fell in her wake.

Olly was straining to pull back, to no avail. His arms were white up to the elbows, numb and starting to ache badly.

Kiran and Tilly grabbed Olly round the waist and pulled. No movement. The white was now between

Olly's elbows and shoulders. They pulled again with no result while above them Liam and Jack leaped dangerously from glass tube to bottle stopper to terminal block across the top of the jumbled apparatus. They got as near as they could to the circle of coils above the Stone but it was still more than a mouse-jump away. Looking round desperately, Liam spotted a length of plastic pipe sticking out of a nearby test-tube. Quickly he and Jack grabbed it and extended it across the gap, making a precarious bridge.

Liam scuttled across while Jack went down to Olly with Liam's tablet, keeping well clear of the freeze area.

'Move wen I say,' the screen said.

Olly nodded, trying to stay calm, but the white had reached his shoulders and he was starting to gasp for breath. Any further and his lungs could totally freeze.

Tilly and Kiran craned to see Liam. He was hard at work gnawing insulation off wire at six points round the circle of coils. Then using some wire he had in his rucksack, he set about cross-connecting three points on one half of the circle with the corresponding three on the other half. Each time he twisted wires together there were sparks and a loud electrical hum. When he came to the last connection, he was fairly sure he would get a fatal shock if he touched the bare wires directly with his paws so he just held them together with his handkerchief.

There was a bang and a smell of burning. The humming sound became continuous and started to go down in pitch.

Deeper and deeper it went until it became a throb they could feel rather than hear. At the same time the advance of white frost towards Olly's neck slowed and finally stopped. Then the pitch of the hum started to rise again and the white tide gradually started to recede down his arms, towards his wrists. The shimmering curtain grew fainter and more transparent. All the time the smell of burning was getting stronger. Liam's handkerchief began to smoulder under his paw.

Jack was looking up anxiously, his arm in the air ready to signal Olly to move when Liam gave the word. Olly's hands were unfreezing and the shimmer was virtually gone.

'Owww,' Liam howled, 'it's too hot to hold on.'

He let go.

The two wires jumped apart with an explosive spark. Liam was catapulted into space.

Jack dropped his arm and shouted 'Move!' in Mouse.

Olly grabbed the Stone and pulled free. Tilly caught Liam like a tennis ball. Kiran staggered back against a table and three bottles fell off.

No-one spoke for a moment.

'That was close,' Liam puffed from Tilly's cupped hands. He mopped his brow with a charred handkerchief, leaving black streaks.

Olly waggled his fingers and flexed his arms. They were fine, apart from some tingling. 'What happened?' he asked, bewildered.

So they could all talk to each other he held the Stone while Tilly and Kiran touched it.

'You were trapped in an anti-phase modulated microwave field,' said Liam, as though it explained everything.

They all looked at him blankly.

'You've heard of microwave ovens?' he asked, blinking as he patiently polished his glasses.

They all nodded.

'They work by crashing molecules together. This is a microwave freezer. It does the opposite.'

'That's a new one on me,' said Jack.

'And me,' said Liam, 'but it's a fantastic idea isn't it? And logical when you think about it. I just reversed the transducer inputs so it switched from chilling to warming. The amazing thing is how it grabbed Olly so he couldn't move. I've no idea how that was done. I had to gamble that it would let him go when it reached room temperature. Fortunately, I was right. Otherwise it would have cooked him.'

26

ALFRED

The children ran out of the laboratory, back up the steps and into Botwulf's room. Daniel lay on his side now, moaning every time he breathed out. He was very hot and sweaty. Fresh blood seeped from his wounds.

'He must have tried to turn over in his sleep,' said Kiran, gulping back a sob, 'we shouldn't have left him alone.'

She discarded her lever weapon and knelt to hold Daniel's hand. They all felt guilty.

'Let's try with the Stone quickly,' said Tilly.

Kiran locked the door from the inside and Tilly told Daniel quietly what they were going to try in case he could hear. Then, sitting by his head, she and Olly both touched the Stone with one hand and Daniel's temples with the other. They closed their eyes and concentrated.

'This is what they did with Ian,' said Liam to Jack from Olly's pocket. Jack's head poked out of Kiran's pocket.

It was different from how it had been with Ian. There was the dream-like vision and thoughts streaming past like water but whereas Ian was living and re-living the minutes before his injury, Daniel's thoughts were a confused tangle. First he was being carried, kicking and struggling, from his room, next he was lying on the black rug, then he was running along the beach, then he was playing football, then he was looking into Boyles shop window, then Heron was flying straight at him, then there was an excruciating pain in his shoulder and he was being strangled, then he was falling, then he was smelling

Botwulf, then he was running along in darkness with his hands tied behind his back, then…

Daniel, can you hear me? Olly asked gently. The flow steadied and slowed. *It's me, Olly. Tilly's here too and Kiran, but you probably can't see her. Can you see me?*

The stream went blurred then refocussed. Before, there had been only the water but now there were banks and they saw Daniel sitting at the water's edge on the other side. It was daylight but the sun was hidden by cloud. Olly waded across.

Hello Olly, said Daniel. *Do you want to play football?*

Daniel, Olly replied, *your back and head are hurt. Tilly and me are going to see if we can put them right.*

As before, Olly's mind and Tilly's had joined into one.

OK, said Daniel, *but watch out for the wolf thing. It gets you round the neck and sticks its claws into you.* As he said it the children's mental picture wobbled.

Olly was beside Daniel on the other bank now and tried to lift him but, as with Ian, the injuries were holding him down. Although Olly and Tilly badly wanted to repair the injuries, they could not see how to do it, no matter how hard they willed it.

Suddenly they had a feeling that they were being watched.

Olly raised his head, eyes still closed, and saw a man in a leather tunic and rough-woven trousers. He was not old but not young either and below dark curly hair, his eyes were a rich, deep blue. Tilly could see him too. He was strangely familiar. They instinctively knew they could trust him. Indeed somehow they knew who it was.

Are you Alfred? Tilly asked with her mind.

Yes, said the man. *You are descended from me.*

We'd like to help Daniel, said Olly. *Can you tell us how? We must hurry because Botwulf may discover at any moment that we have taken the Stone.*

You are right, time is short, said Alfred. *You must get to work. The injuries are serious.*

While this was going on, Daniel had been throwing pebbles into the water, apparently not paying any attention to the conversation.

Look at your minds, said Alfred.

What do you mean..., they began but immediately something like a mental somersault took place in their heads and they found they could look inwards to see the workings of their own minds, especially a place of healing there that they realised they must have unconsciously used on Ian. As they looked they recognised how it could be switched on and controlled.

Turning their attention back to Daniel, they now understood all his injuries as though they were doctors. Quite apart from the deep wounds on his back, filth from Curwald's claws and tongue had infected Daniel's blood and would soon cause irreversible damage to his heart, lungs and brain. Worse still, there was a fracture of the skull and swelling of the brain beneath. His temperature was impossibly high and he was in a coma. Daniel would die if nothing was done.

Systematically they used the power of their joined minds on each of the injuries in turn, focussing on repairing the damage and restoring Daniel to health. It was more complicated than dealing with Ian and took an intense effort of concentration but when they had finished, Daniel was sleeping peacefully, a smile on his face.

Kiran had heard nothing but knew that something was going on. Olly and Tilly were silent, eyes shut, yet she noticed a big change in Daniel.

Well done, children, said Alfred.

But we still don't know how we can do it, they said, *or how we can see you.*

The Stone releases your mind's strength. It is in you and all our family. You see me because the Stone connects us through time.

How can we stop Odric?

He will rise at midnight. You will be forced once again to part with the Stone. There is nothing to be done to prevent it. Indeed it could be dangerous to interfere.

Why?

There is no time to explain now, for Botwulf has sensed the Stone being used and is returning even as I speak. Just remember that once Odric is risen, he will become vulnerable like all men. Stay close to him because he must then be destroyed.

You mean we should kill him? asked Olly, suddenly feeling frightened and not sure that they could.

Your power grows in proportion to the evil you face, said Alfred. *It will grow further yet…*

An explosion blew the door off its hinges, its shockwave sending the children sprawling. Botwulf burst in through the smoke.

27

WHACK!

As darkness fell Heron and Wickfeather returned briefly from patrol to check for developments. They had ranged widely up and down the coast and several miles inland but had nothing to report. Heron was sleek and preened, having had access to plenty of fish oil.

Ian had kept regular radio contact with S.S. Dauntless, which at present was just off Whitby lighthouse. The Captain reported that all was quiet apart from the weather which continued stormy. Gales were forecast for later in the night.

The news from underground, or rather the lack of it, including the abortive geophone call, was received solemnly by them all.

'I've sent the Mole Commandos in,' Aristotle confided to Wickfeather over a cup of dandelion tea as they looked at some ancient parchments on the control room table. 'The librarians dug out these old maps and we took a guess at where the children might be. As far as I can see the tunnel goes roughly northwards, and combining what we know from The First Book with what Ian saw, I'm gambling on their being somewhere underneath the Abbey.'

'That seems a logical conclusion,' said Wickfeather after studying the maps.

Ian had been sitting at a control panel with a headset, speaking occasionally into the microphone. He moved one earphone aside and turned to Aristotle and Wickfeather.

'Disturbance in the tunnel between the phone box

and the Boyles' shop,' he reported. 'Listen.'

He flicked a switch and a loudspeaker came on. Something was barking in Dog, including what sounded suspiciously like swear words.

'Jess!' they all said at once.

'Quickly,' said Aristotle, 'we must get her here.'

Ian looked worried. 'She went down through Daniel's bedroom but we can't use that entrance to get her out, for obvious reasons,' he said. 'The only other entrance we know that's large enough for a dog is in the Boyles' shop. It would mean breaking into the shop, which I suppose is no problem as we know that the sisters and Meanwhisker aren't there, but how would we lift the stone slab? It's too heavy for us small creatures. We need a human to do it.'

'Leave this to me,' said Aristotle, crossing the room to a computer. Quickly, he logged on and sent a message.

I just hope he's there, he thought.

Luckily, he was. The reply was immediate and typically brief: 'On my way.'

Minutes later Aristotle and Ian met the recipient of the message in a dark alley behind the sweetshop.

'Good evening, Mr Regdab,' said the Colonel as he and Aristotle shook hands. Ian, amazed, translated the greeting into Rabbit. Aristotle explained that the two had known each other for many years but had kept it a secret, so they rarely met in person but there was absolute trust between them.

Ian introduced himself using the screen of his tablet.

'Hello,' said the Colonel. 'Shall we proceed?' Without further ado he used his elbow to smash a pane of glass in the Boyles' back door, put his arm through and released the catch. Within seconds, they were in the unlit shop, lifting the stone slab. Jess bounded out enthusiastically.

'About time,' she said in Rabbit. Aristotle ducked to

avoid her joyfully swiping tail and Ian dashed under the counter to keep out of the way of her prancing feet. The Colonel was very pleased to see her. He stroked her head and neck with both hands and clapped her warmly on the back.

'Back to my place?' asked the Colonel. They needed to talk so it seemed a good idea, especially as it was so close.

In the Colonel's cosy living room, it took Ian only a moment to connect his tablet to the Colonel's computer and as Jess told them all she knew, a translation appeared on the Colonel's monitor.

Jess's audience was aghast at her account of the pit, Daniel's injuries and Olly being knocked out in the fight with Botwulf and the sisters.

'If you ask me, those sisters aren't human,' said Jess. 'Their blood isn't right.'

'Time I got ready,' said the Colonel, standing up decisively.

Aristotle got up too.

'You are willing to go down, then?' he asked via Ian and the computer.

The Colonel gave a smart salute.

'At your service,' he said crisply.

On Aristotle's instructions Ian, even more amazed, typed 'Good Luck!' in capital letters on the Colonel's screen.

The animals left and the Colonel set about his preparations.

***

The explosion disorientated the children and caused Olly and Tilly to let go of the Stone. Dense, acrid smoke billowed everywhere. It hurt their nostrils and the backs of their throats, making them cough. They could not see each other and their ears were numbed by the blast.

Daniel woke up coughing but felt much better. He was lying on a black rug and the room was full of smoke. His head did not hurt and he could tell that the wounds on his back had gone. He sat up.

'Is anyone there?' he asked tremulously. He felt nervous but his strength was returning.

'Yes, me,' said Kiran from somewhere in the fog, happy to hear his voice again.

If we could find the Stone, thought Tilly, *we could escape with it under the smokescreen.*

How did you say that? asked Olly. Neither of them had the Stone.

'So, you stupid children, you try my patience yet again.' Botwulf's voice startled them all.

Now on their knees, Olly and Tilly could hazily make out his dark, bent shape. They were feeling around on the floor for the Stone.

'Looking for this?' asked Botwulf triumphantly. The tone of his voice was even more unbearable than usual. He came nearer and they could see that he was holding the Stone.

He got that quickly, thought Olly.

Yes but we're communicating without it! Tilly replied. *What shall we do? Fight or go?*

Whack!

Before they could think or stand up something hit Botwulf from behind and he catapulted forward. His smell briefly enveloped them as he shot between them to fall full length on the rug.

'I needed that,' said Daniel. He appeared out of the smoke brandishing the wooden lever in both hands like a baseball bat.

'Run!' he shouted.

Botwulf still gripped the Stone, too precious for him

to let go. Olly and Tilly thought in unison: Alfred had said they should not stop it from being used to raise Odric.

They left it and raced for the door. Daniel was ahead of them.

'Right with you,' shouted a figure in the mist – Kiran, sweeping up the rucksack as she went.

Botwulf picked himself up and cursed. Those idiotic children caused nothing but trouble. He had been surprised rather than hurt by Daniel's blow and had managed to hold on to the Stone. Now the children had run away, but no matter. As soon as he had found the Stone the mental chatter between them had ceased. They could do nothing now. He had the Stone and would not part with it again. He must return with it to the laboratory – there was just enough time before midnight to complete his work. After midnight the children would be irrelevant. His Master's power would see to that.

28

ODRIC

On reaching the main tunnel, the children turned left and ran towards the village.

'Stop a minute,' said Olly, panting, when they were about half way to the pit. 'Let's just see if he's following.'

They stopped and held their breath to listen. No sound behind.

'He's only thinking about Stone not us,' whispered Tilly, 'but still we'd better be quiet.'

They continued towards the pit, hoping the lever they had moved had closed it but when they got there their hopes were dashed. Curwald smelled them and growled longingly, making Daniel shudder at the memory of his encounter.

'Thanks for making me better,' he said to Olly and Tilly. 'How did you do it?'

'Well, we had some practice with a mouse called Ian,' said Olly

'Was I more difficult to deal with than him?'

'No,' said Kiran. 'A mouse is a lot more complicated than you because its brain can think about other things than football.' Liam chuckled in Olly's pocket.

'Welcome back from the jaws of death, Daniel,' said Daniel to Kiran, trying to sound as if he was in a huff. 'And thanks for knocking Botwulf over so we could all escape.' It wasn't that funny but they all laughed – it relieved the tension.

Olly explained about the help from Alfred. Kiran and Daniel were amazed.

'It was like he was standing next to us.' said Tilly.

She also told them it was now pretty certain that Odric would awaken at midnight.

'So we, that is Olly and me, need to be nearby when it happens but the rest of you don't and maybe it would be better for you to try getting back to the village.'

'How?' said Kiran scathingly. 'Just jump over the pit I suppose.'

'We wondered about that shaft,' said Olly quietly.

'Oh yes,' said Kiran, remembering the horrible smell.

'What shaft?' asked Daniel.

'You were having a sleep when the rest of us saw it,' said Kiran. Daniel aimed a blow at her but she sidestepped. 'It's near Botwulf's laboratory, at the bottom of the steps.'

'If you can't get up it,' Olly continued, 'just wait by the pit because if Jess has got through there may be reinforcements coming down. If they do we need to warn them not to do anything until after midnight because of what Alfred said about not stopping Odric waking up.'

'What if we do get up the shaft though?' said Kiran. 'What do we say to Mum and Dad and everyone?'

They all realised it would be just too complicated to explain the full facts. Eventually, at Liam's suggestion, it was decided they should get straight in touch with Aristotle. He would know what to do.

Liam, standing up in Olly's pocket, said via the tablet that he'd better stay to help Olly and Tilly. Jack was deputed to go with Kiran and Daniel so he could explain things to Aristotle.

'It'll be dangerous for all of us,' said Tilly seriously.

Liam believed her. She and her brother had been different, more subdued, in the short time since they had used the Stone to heal Daniel. Liam felt scared and his knees were trembling a bit but fortunately they were below the pocket-line so no one could see. There was no going back though. He had to stay to protect them if he could.

Kiran took the rucksack but they divided the food between them first. Olly kept his torch and as an afterthought the scissors.

They tiptoed in silence back the way they had come and stopped when they reached the heavy door, ears straining to catch the faintest sound of Botwulf or the sisters.

Jack scampered quietly along the passage, heart in mouth for fear of meeting Meanwhisker, to check Botwulf's room but came back to report it empty. They presumed Botwulf and the sisters were down in the laboratory.

With that the Petersons and the Akrams parted company.

Olly and Tilly walked quietly down the main tunnel and the Akrams went towards the steps.

***

This communicating without the Stone, sent Tilly as they walked, *must be our powers growing as Alfred said.*

I'm not sure about that because you're not nearly as loud as you were when we were escaping just now. Do you notice the same with me?

They agreed that the strength of the thoughts they received from one another was waning.

They continued down the tunnel and the further they went the weaker the thoughts became. Gradually, it became more and more difficult to receive them. They finally reverted to whispers because it took less effort.

'Maybe we can only do it temporarily, after we've been using the Stone,' suggested Tilly. 'Perhaps it sort of wears off.'

These words were the first Liam had heard for quite a while, so he popped his head and tablet out of the pocket and asked what they were talking about. The children explained and Liam was relieved to know they had been exchanging thoughts. The silence had been worrying.

Olly admitted that Tilly could be right, but he had been thinking. 'Suppose that the strength of the thoughts depends on how near we are to the Stone.'

'Cud be,' said Liam to his tablet.

'Mm,' replied Tilly, 'If Botwulf's in his laboratory with it we're moving away from him all the time.'

'We could test it by going back a bit,' said Olly. They began cautiously to retrace their steps. Sure enough, the further they went the stronger the thoughts became.

Experiment over, they turned round again and headed towards the Scar Tomb, soon coming to a dead end.

'This must be where the entrance is,' said Olly. 'According to Ian you touch the wall and the door opens.'

They felt all over the walls but nothing happened.

'It's all fairly smooth apart from this lump here,' said Tilly after a while. She grasped it and felt it lift at the bottom. It was a hinged flap behind which was a handle that operated the door.

It swung open smoothly.

An awful sense of dread came upon them as they felt evil escaping from inside. Liam felt it too. It brought on knee wobbles.

They peeped in and saw a great cavern with a faintly luminous roof that gave off just enough light to see the oblong plinth that Ian had seen with – something – on it. The smell was dreadful. They slipped through the door and sidled along the wall, crouching low in case anyone was there but the place was deserted apart from the something. They closed the door gently behind them with a concealed handle like the one on the outside. Black trunks and packing cases stood round the edge of the cavern. They were open as though someone had been unpacking and to one side of the plinth an area was laid out like a furnished room with a carpet, chairs, a table and a bookcase.

'Let's take a closer look at Odric,' said Olly.

They quietly crossed the chamber to the plinth. The sense of evil intensified as they approached it. The sight of Odric was every bit as hideous and chilling as Ian's story had led them to expect and, like Ian, it made all three of them want to run away, but they knew they must not. Liam took one look and retreated to the bottom of Olly's pocket.

Odric was bound by chains round his ankles, wrists and neck. The chains were long enough to allow him some movement but not enough to turn over or sit upright. His eyes were shut but he was restless, pulling first at one chain, then another, sometimes moaning, sometimes shouting unintelligible words.

He wore the remains of a ragged black habit with most of his chest and upper body exposed. He would be very tall if he stood up. His dark grey skin was flaky, almost scaly. It was covered in sores, dripping blood and yellow matter, which, together with evil smelling bile from his bowels, ran into a channel and disappeared down a drain hole. It was all impossibly revolting.

The two children walked right round the plinth. It was jet black and the sides featureless except for a round indentation at the foot end that was smooth inside and several centimetres deep. It had no obvious purpose but when Tilly touched it some numbers flashed on above it for a moment and made her jump.

'What's that?' she said in a startled whisper.

Olly tried it and the same thing happened but the numbers didn't look quite the same. After a couple more tries Liam said 'Countdown,' to his tablet.

He was right. It showed 2:12. Olly's watch said 9.48 pm. Just over two hours to midnight.

The smell was too bad to be near Odric for long so they retired to the edge of the room where the atmosphere was a little less unpleasant.

They ate some food, giving Liam cheese, then chose two empty trunks side by side to hide in. They used the scissors to make small holes for air and to see out of, after which they closed the lids and settled down to wait. They were close enough to have a whispered conversation.

'What do you think will happen at midnight and what about — afterwards?' asked Tilly. Neither of them had spoken of the dreadful responsibility Alfred had placed on them but each knew that it weighed heavily on the other.

'Well, I suppose Odric will wake up,' replied Olly, 'and Botwulf will have some way of removing the chains. As to afterwards — I just don't know. We haven't got a bomb or a gun, or a knife, or anything to destroy him with as Alfred put it. He didn't reply when you asked if that meant killing him but I think it must. I don't see how we can though — all we've got is the scissors.'

As he said the word *kill* his stomach twisted with fear. Tilly, too, felt the chilling mood grip her more tightly. The bleak exchange of words made Liam feel dismal and alone. All three knew in their hearts that they did not have it in them to kill in cold blood.

29

WHOOSH!

Daniel and Kiran, with Jack still in her kite-pocket, crept through the doorway from the main tunnel, along the passage and down the steps. The door on the other side of the cavern was almost shut and they could hear muffled voices in the laboratory. The square opening into the shaft was at the children's waist level and just large enough for them to lean into it side by side. It went through about half a metre of rock.

The updraught was quite strong and the smell it carried so bad it made their noses sting and their eyes water. They flashed their torch round the shaft. The walls were smooth rock and there seemed to be no way to climb up. Kiran turned to lean backwards into the shaft for a better view up it. Daniel held her feet.

From that angle she could see iron rungs forming a ladder, set into the wall above the opening.

As she withdrew from the opening the updraught caught a flap of the kite, hanging from her pocket, and whipped it into the shaft. The rest of the kite followed, streaking upwards with tangled string trailing behind it. Inside the pocket a loop caught Jack neatly round the waist. One moment he was safe and snug, the next he was shooting up the shaft. Kiran tried to grab the string but missed – and it was gone, Jack with it. He did not even have time to cry out. None of them had uttered a sound.

Kiran and Daniel looked at each other horror-struck. They shone the torch up the shaft but kite, string and Jack were already out of sight.

'What are we going to do?' whispered Kiran, tears forming in her eyes. 'It's all my fault.'

Daniel felt like crying too but suddenly voices from the laboratory became louder as the door was pushed open. They did not wait to see if anyone came out. They ran for the steps.

***

Jack was very, very scared but had no time to think about it. As he shot up the shaft, adrenaline pumped round his tiny body as it had never pumped before. He did not want to go up the shaft but now that he was, he certainly did not want to fall down. The string round his waist was part of a tangled ball. Was it knotted or just a loose loop that might release him at any moment? He grabbed the ball and hung on to as much of the string as he could, using both hands and both feet.

The ascending kite spun crazily, weaving from side to side. Jack was tossed around like a leaf in the wind. It made him dizzy. He felt sick and was in danger of banging against the walls of the shaft but he did not let go. It had nothing to do with rational thought. His mind and body were gripped in a single survival reflex.

Up and up he flew, in total darkness. He tried to see what was above him but all was blackness. He looked down. That, too, was black. Then he became aware of a sound. A rushing, roaring noise, getting louder and louder. It seemed familiar but his mind was concentrated on holding on, which stopped him identifying it.

With a sudden *whoosh*, he was in the open air. It was night, he was still going up and the warmth of the updraught gave way to cold, salty wind and driving rain. Below him, boiling surf. The sea! The noise he had heard was the sea.

He saw that he had shot out of the ground near the

top of a cliff and now continued to spiral upwards. Wind and rain beat against him and seemed to reduce the spinning of the kite. He looked down. He could see the lights of a town and a ruined building with floodlights. Whitby Abbey! But he was flying out to sea away from it on the strong north-westerly and the kite, now made heavy by the rain, was starting to lose height. As he descended and left the land behind, the Abbey seemed both to rise out of the sea and shrink at the same time.

Looking down, he saw the water approaching with terrifying speed.

Splash! He hit the freezing sea hard and went under with a shocked intake of breath, swallowing a lot of water. He let go of the string but was still tangled in it. Choking and coughing and taking water into his lungs in his panic, he tried to swim upwards but every movement of his arms and legs wrapped the wet string more tightly around him. He tried to hold his breath but more bitter seawater came through his nose, and still he went down.

He was dizzy, weak and freezing. There was no more adrenaline. He stopped struggling. His mind became calm and began to drift. He knew that he did not want to die but at the same time he knew he was drowning. Funny, he thought, drowning's the last thing I expected when I went down the tunnels with the children. Isn't life strange? Death will be even stranger, probably.

Here it comes too, he thought, because I'm going up. I must be going to heaven. That's something at least. Above him was a blurred image of wings.

An angel, he thought. I'd better be on my best behaviour.

30

S.S. DAUNTLESS

This is no night for any self-respecting bird to be on the wing, thought Heron, as he battled up the coast in fierce winds. The sea was churned into a frenzy. Spray flew upwards. Rain drove horizontally. Gravity seemed to have lost its grip. He had to work hard to keep a straight course, constantly blown to one side or the other, or plummeting in a downdraught.

Salt in the air is making my back feathers all sticky, he grumbled to himself, but there were matters at stake more important than back feathers. Aristotle was relying on him and Wickfeather to patrol the area. All the same, he thought, I'd better keep my fish oil levels up, and dropped a little to scan the surface of the sea for signs of fish.

Dauntless Arvicola, his ship coping well with the stormy seas, had been feeling lonely out there in the deteriorating weather.

There was a thump on the wheelhouse roof and a long beak with a beady eye above it poked down through the open door.

'H-Hello Heron,' said Dauntless Arvicola, startled. 'Wh-what are you doing here,?'

'You might have said, 'Hello, nice to see you,'' said Heron, feeling rather short tempered.

'W-well it is,' replied Dauntless Arvicola, his nose blushing, 'b-but you arrived so s-suddenly I hadn't t-time to th-think.'

'Hmm,' said Heron and hopped off the roof into the wheelhouse. 'In answer to your question, I've just stopped off for a rest. I don't suppose you've got any fish?'

Dauntless Arvicola shook his head. 'N-nuts, though,' he said enthusiastically.

Heron muttered something inaudible, waddled out of the wheelhouse and took off in search of fish.

A couple of hundred metres from the boat, he saw a splash and went down to investigate. There was string floating on the water, probably a broken fishing line, and some torn fragments of plastic. That wouldn't be heavy enough to make a splash, thought Heron. Maybe there's a fish on the line. With a beating of wings he grabbed the string and flew upwards, pulling it out of the water. There was definitely something on the end of it.

He flew back towards the boat. Dauntless Arvicola, well protected in yellow oilskins, was watching. He could hardly believe what he saw.

'Not a fish,' said Heron disgustedly as he landed on the deck.

'N-no, it's J-Jack,' said Dauntless Arvicola, struggling to release him from the string.

Jack was limp and grey, his eyes closed. He was not breathing. Instinctively, Dauntless Arvicola turned him into the Rodent Recovery Position and began chest compressions. The procedure was drummed into all young voles at an early age, for drowning is the most common danger they face.

Water flooded out of Jack's mouth and nose, as Dauntless Arvicola worked on the small body. Heron, fish forgotten, spread his wings to shelter them from the icy wind and rain.

Dauntless Arvicola continued a sequence of massage and chest compressions for a full minute. No response. Another half minute. Still nothing. It was worrying. He should be showing signs of life by now. Dauntless

Arvicola was beginning to give up hope when he thought he saw a slight movement in Jack's chest. He redoubled his efforts and almost at once was rewarded with a retching cough as Jack threw up more water, spluttered and began to breathe again.

Heron was so pleased he hugged Dauntless Arvicola with his wings.

Dauntless Arvicola, his nose bright pink with delight and embarrassment, carefully carried Jack into the main cabin and laid him gently on one of the seats with a pillow and two blankets. He turned up the heating and in the small galley put the kettle on to make a hot drink. He was fully prepared because next to drowning, hypothermia is the biggest killer of aquatic rodents.

Gradually, Jack's breathing settled down and warmth began to return to his body. He opened his eyes.

I'm glad heaven's warm and they have beds, he thought dreamily, as he looked at the feathery angel standing beside him. Soon another angel, but with no feathers and looking rather like a vole, helped him drink a cup of steaming dandelion tea sweetened with three lumps of sugar.

Jack was a strong young mouse and it was not long before he was sitting up and they were all laughing about him thinking Heron was an angel. He was obviously going to make a full recovery. There was no cheese on the ship but some of the Captain's nuts put strength back into him and he briefed them on the situation in the tunnels. Dauntless Arvicola wasted no time getting on the radio to Section H.Q.

In the control room, Ian and Aristotle could hardly believe their ears when they heard of Jack's amazing flight up the shaft.

'That's one for the history books,' said Ian.

Relieved as they were that Jack had survived, they

were concerned at the other news he brought and also amazed that Alfred had appeared to Olly and Tilly.

'I'm worried about the message that Odric should be allowed to rise,' said Aristotle with furrowed brow. 'I've already sent in the Mole Commandos to recover the Stone if they can. Are we in touch with them, Ian?'

Ian shook his head. 'I'm afraid not. No radio contact underground and they don't have geophones. And anyway we already know that geophones are a bit iffy down there.'

'I must consult with the Colonel,' said Aristotle, sitting down at the computer to send him a message.

In his cottage the Colonel had only one item of preparation left. He and Jess would be leaving in a few minutes. He checked his messages prior to turning off the computer, hesitating for barely a moment before sending a reply to Aristotle.

'Advice of A almost certainly correct. Will not strike before midnight but will get into position beforehand. Will look out for Moles.'

***

The Colonel's uniform had for some years been hanging in a plastic bag in his wardrobe. It was still as smart and well pressed as the day he put it away. He put it on and surveyed himself in the mirror.

'Must look my best,' he muttered under his breath. 'Mustn't let the family down.'

Downstairs he sealed an envelope and left it propped up on a small table by the window. Calling Jess to follow, he shouldered a military pack, put a revolver in his holster and stepped quietly into the street, locking the door behind him. The thick rubber soles of his SAS boots made virtually no sound on the ground. Training and attention to detail had eliminated any rattle or click from his equipment. Stealth was an important weapon on secret missions. He and Jess felt at ease. Just like old times in the army.

So effective was their use of shadow and camouflage that not a single person saw them go to the Boyles' shop, from where they entered the tunnel.

***

'I wonder when those children are coming home?' said Granny to her husband from the kitchen. 'The searching has stopped for the night. They should be back by now.'

Bill Peterson was sitting by the fire.

'Probably gone to the Akrams,' he said, burying his head in the newspaper.

The telephone rang. Fortunately he got there first.

'Is Kiran with you?' asked Mrs Akram.

'Yes,' he lied, wondering how he was going to deal with the conversation.

'Well, will you send her home soon?' said Mrs Akram.

'Just had tea and invited to stay the night,' he said. For his wife's benefit he tried to sound as though he was repeating what Mrs Akram said. 'Is that alright with you?'

'No problem,' said Mrs Akram. 'It'll probably do her good to be with her friends…' Her voice tailed off and Bill Peterson knew that she was crying silently.

'Courage,' he said. 'There'll be a big search tomorrow. The situation could be very different in twenty four hours.' He knew it could be worse rather than better but he wanted to spare Mrs Akram's feelings.

'Thank you, Mr Peterson, you are a good man,' sobbed Mrs Akram. 'Goodbye.'

'Did you hear that, dear?' Bill Peterson asked his wife.

'Yes, staying the night at the Akrams,' she replied. 'It'll probably do them good to have someone else in the house.'

Phew, he thought, I only just managed that.

***

Ingrid emerged from Botwulf's laboratory as Kiran and Daniel were racing unseen up the steps. As they reached the top they heard her calling for Meanwhisker, then Botwulf calling after her.

'Make sure you find the idiot creature. We need it for our experiment.'

Running as quietly as they could, Kiran and Daniel went straight to the pit. There was nothing for it but to wait there.

They had never felt so wretched. They were certain Jack was dead and they were responsible. How could they ever live with themselves or face Liam and the others again. They sat silently against the wall, sad, cold and despondent.

31

POWER

Tilly opened her eyes and stared. She was in bed at her grandparents' cottage but something had woken her. She could not see the something because of the darkness but she knew that it was there for she felt cold evil coming to get her. She sat up, eyes searching the blackness, panic choking her throat. She thrust out her arms to ward off whatever was there then pulled them back because she did not want to touch it. Her scream, when it came, was thin and high pitched, full of the fear that surrounded and engulfed her. Olly and Liam heard it and leapt out of their trunk. Tilly heard it too. It woke her up.

Olly swung open the lid of Tilly's trunk. In the dim light he and Liam saw her huddled in a corner, knees drawn up to her chin. She was shivering with fright and beads of sweat stood out on her forehead. Her eyes stared, wide open, still full of nightmare visions. It was a few moments before she began to see properly again, responding to their words of reassurance.

Olly wanted to say, 'Don't worry it's just a dream, everything's OK,' like their mother used to when they had night terrors as small children but everything was not OK and they had plenty to worry about and the worst part of it was that it was not a dream.

It's just the nearness of Odric affecting you, sent Olly.

'That's right,' said Liam, 'it's enough to give anyone the heebie jeebies.'

Tilly's mind muttered something incoherent, then suddenly woke up to the fact that they were exchanging thoughts. In the same moment Liam realised he could understand the children just as if they had spoken while holding the Stone.

Quick, hide. Botwulf must be coming, Tilly sent, so loudly it made Olly and Liam wince. Yet something made her pause and Olly paused too. Their minds, virtually one, scanned the surrounding area in a way that they had not previously been able to.

No, I don't think he is coming, is he? they thought to each other. *We can tell the Stone's in his laboratory and he's there with it.*

'How?' asked Liam, amazed. He was standing on the edge of the trunk, hand on catpin, ready either to draw it or to jump into a pocket as occasion demanded.

We don't know, they sent, *but we think Botwulf's likely to stay there for a little while. It's not like seeing his thoughts, more like looking along the path of time he's going to follow. We can't see beyond midnight, though.*

Olly looked at his watch: Twenty minutes to go. Both children were surprised. They must have been asleep.

'Yes, you were,' said Liam, 'and I was catnapping too.' Mice use the term to mean snoozing with one eye open for cats. 'By the way, if I can hear what you're thinking, surely Botwulf can too?'

That's a point, Tilly sent. The children fell silent and looked at their own minds as Alfred had taught them. It was like studying a map.

No, he can't, can he? thought Olly after a moment. Tilly agreed. *If we wanted him to hear we could let him but we don't and our minds know it so they shut him out.*

'Like a settings menu on a computer program?' asked Liam

Sort of, they replied.

After Tilly's nightmare they agreed that Liam would go into her trunk to keep her company while they waited.

'For what?' Liam wondered out loud.

We don't know, came the reply.

Very comforting, I don't think, thought Liam.

***

The wind had been rising all evening and was now at gale force, whipping up the sea and causing immense breakers to crash against the sea wall. Rain beat horizontally against the tiny village houses. Bill Peterson lay awake listening to it all and worrying about the children.

Sometimes he worried about the village, too. In 1780, part of it had collapsed down the cliff. It could happen again.

Wickfeather continued his patrol. He was used to flying in all conditions.

The *SS Dauntless* was designed to ride out storms but the Captain needed all his strength and skill to keep the bows facing into the wind. Heron, recently fortified with a fish supper, was beside him in the wheelhouse, acting as lookout. He preferred not to fly in such conditions. In the comfortable cabin, Jack was sleeping.

In the control room at Section H.Q., Aristotle and Ian sat quietly.

'I should have gone with the Colonel,' said Aristotle after a while.

'The Council expressly forbade it,' said Ian. 'Wickfeather told me. It's me who should have gone.

'Dr Quick expressly forbade it,' said Aristotle.

'Liam's still down there,' Ian went on. 'If anything happens to him I'll never forgive myself. I'll go scatty just sitting here waiting for news but it's no use setting off now. We'd never catch the Colonel up. I presume the others are somewhere near the bottom of the shaft Jack flew out of and if that's near Whitby Abbey it's several miles away as the crow flies, probably further by tunnel.'

Aristotle agreed. 'I asked Wickfeather to keep an eye open for the top of the shaft but what with the darkness and this weather there isn't much chance of seeing it. Even if he found it *we* couldn't get there without sprouting wings.'

Suddenly, Ian sat up. 'Who says?' he asked.

***

Curwald paced around the pit growling. Kiran and Daniel had become used to the sound and their ears ignored it. They had no idea what time it was. Daniel, exhausted by his ordeals, was asleep.

The Colonel and Jess made almost no sound. They stopped short of the pit on hearing Curwald and the first Kiran knew of their arrival was a low growl from Jess and a quick flash of torchlight.

'Hello, is someone there?' she shouted.

Daniel was instantly awake.

'Foster,' came the staccato reply.

Kiran and Daniel looked at each other. The Colonel! What was he doing here? They still did not know whose side he was on.

In his backpack, the Colonel had brought some metal spars that fitted together in sections to form a narrow bridge. Soon he had crossed the pit, further enraging Curwald.

'Nasty piece of work,' said the Colonel, looking down at the wolf. 'Jess told me.' In a few short phrases he brought the children up to date with events on the surface.

They were amazed and overjoyed to hear that Jack was alive after all and relieved that the Colonel was on their side. They were pleased to see Jess again, too. She wagged her tail energetically.

'I suppose you know that we have to let Odric rise at

midnight,' said Kiran importantly, 'but after that we can do anything we like.'

The Colonel assured her that he was fully up to speed and that the plan was both to put Odric out of action and rescue the Petersons.

'Liam, too,' said Kiran.

The Colonel nodded and looked at his watch. Almost a quarter to twelve.

'Fifteen minutes,' he said. 'Then I go in. Children – back up to the village.'

'And miss all the fun,' said Kiran, 'you must be joking.' She was feeling much safer now and anxious to do something to help. Daniel, too, was warming to the prospect of getting back at Botwulf.

The Colonel looked them in the eye for a moment and they looked defiantly back. He made a decision.

'Big danger,' he said. 'No picnic. Uncertain outcome. Tag along. Follow orders. Without question. No matter what. Understood?'

The children had not seen the Colonel in command mode before. He was rather forceful.

'Understood,' they said meekly. Jess licked their hands in turn. She had a pretty good idea what had been said. She would look after them.

32

POWER FAILURE

They're coming, said Tilly, back in the trunk. Olly sensed it too. Botwulf and the Boyle sisters were approaching with the Stone.

'Any sign of Meanwhisker?' asked Liam, trying to sound calm.

There's a creature or creatures of some sort just out of range but we can't make out what. It seemed to Liam that most of the messages he received were now coming from the children jointly.

I expect that increases the power, he thought.

We think so, too, came their comment.

Mousetraps, thought Liam, if they can read my mind when I'm not speaking, I'd better be careful what I think.

Here they come.

Liam sucked in his whiskers to give his teeth something to do.

From within the trunks, the children could see most of the huge chamber through the holes they had made. The rock door opened and a swarm of bats, led by Wartwing, skimmed silently through, rising to circle like a black cloud high up in the roof. Shortly after them the bent form of Botwulf glided in followed obediently by the sisters. The door slammed shut behind them.

Olly glanced at the time. Five minutes to midnight.

'Master, your time is come,' said Botwulf, his cracked and rasping voice attempting to sound triumphant. 'Behold the Stone.'

As he spoke, Botwulf produced the Stone from the folds of his ragged cloak and held it out with both hands towards the black plinth. The sisters twittered and fidgeted behind him.

Odric had been restless the whole time the children had been in the chamber but stillness now came upon him, as though the presence of the Stone gave him certainty of salvation.

Botwulf advanced to the plinth, Stone held aloft. The bats wheeled in a tight column above it, sensing and drinking in its power. Botwulf walked three times around the plinth, all the time holding out the Stone towards Odric who now stirred and moaned but not in the violent, aggressive way he had done before. The sounds were sighs of satisfaction and the movements a languorous stretching, as he basked in whatever emanated from the Stone.

The children and Liam felt it too but it was not the agreeable sensation that Odric was clearly enjoying. It was the opposite.

All the evil that Odric had previously exuded seemed magnified and deepened. It surrounded them like a mind-numbing thick black wall. Not passive and inanimate, but alive, teeming with every foul form of life or death that anyone had ever imagined, slithering and climbing over one another. All united in a common purpose to close in, corrupt and kill. It sapped their confidence, making them feel helpless, hopeless and depressed.

With an effort of will the children joined their minds to try to protect themselves and Liam. They found they could build a mental barrier to meet and equal the strength of the wall of evil. At once all three began to feel better.

Liam had almost bitten through his whiskers at the first onslaught of the foul wall but as the children built the mental cocoon, his heart began to thump a little less and curiosity glued his eye to his own small hole in Tilly's trunk.

Botwulf moved to the foot of the plinth and lowered the Stone.

Of course, the children thought, *it fits that indentation we found. Grandpa was right – it's a key.*

Botwulf inserted the Stone into the hole and at once numbers appeared in red fire above the plinth counting down the seconds until midnight. 13, 12, 11…

It seemed to the children that every creature in the cavern was holding its breath – Botwulf, the sisters and themselves – even the bats were still, clinging to the roof. Only the body on the plinth continued to move and sigh with pleasure at its imminent liberation.

3, 2, 1…

Botwulf twisted the Stone in its socket and stood back.

A faint rumbling began below the plinth, gradually becoming louder until it was not only a deep sound but also a vibration that shook the floor of the cave. Thin columns of smoke shot out horizontally from the sides of the plinth, turning to jets of flame that rose at the tips and curled upwards until they formed an archway of fire over Odric.

The brightness was startling in the previously dull light. Most of the bats flittered away from it into the darker corners of the cavern. Some of them, the children noted, were a different shape from the rest and hung in the air like small black parachutes…

They *were* small black parachutes and they were not hanging, they were coming down. The Mole-Major and his platoon had broken through the roof in a daring assault to recover the Stone.

It must have been them who were out of range a few minutes ago, said the children in a flash.

'They're a bit late to recover the Stone,' whispered Liam.

What if they try, though, the children thought. *If they pull it out now, it might stop Odric rising, which mustn't happen according to Alfred. Let's send the Mole-Major a message.*

But they could not. The wall of evil prevented messages escaping.

Like a movie on fast forward they watched as the Mole-Major and the eight members of his platoon hit the ground running, straight towards the foot of the plinth, discarding their parachutes as they went. Botwulf, intent on his Master's rising, did not see them until the Mole-Major and his First Lieutenant reached the place where the Stone protruded from its hole. The rest of the platoon fanned out in a defensive circle, backs to the plinth, their small but powerful rifles pointing outwards.

'Noooo,' screamed Botwulf, thirteen centuries of hope on the verge of being dashed. Too late, he lunged forward in a vain attempt to prevent the inevitable. The two moles twisted the Stone in its socket and pulled it out.

There was an angry roar from the not yet conscious Odric, as the flames sputtered and died. The sisters, who up to then had been spellbound by the fiery spectacle, let out a shrill scream.

The Stone was almost the size of a mole, so the two officers held it in a sling between them and ran for the cave edge while Botwulf and the sisters gave chase. The rest of the platoon, moving at great speed, placed themselves between pursuers and pursued in a tactical retreat, sometimes firing over their shoulders, sometimes dropping on one knee to take careful aim.

Botwulf took one mole-bullet through his right ear and another other in the left knee. They made him very angry. As for the sisters, the mole-marksmen aimed for their existing wounds to gain maximum effect. Ingrid gave up the pursuit early, hopping and screeching in pain as she was struck on her bitten ankle, while Astrid now ran in small circles, wailing and waving her wrist about.

There were mole casualties. One was badly injured when Botwulf trod on him and two others sustained head injuries when Astrid picked them up and threw them to the ground but with the help of their comrades they and the remainder of the platoon reached cover behind the boxes and trunks.

Olly and Tilly had so far been too shocked to react. The Mole operation had taken them and everyone by surprise. It had been brilliantly executed but unfortunately was the wrong thing to do. Odric's rising had been stopped and according to Alfred there would be serious consequences.

What now?

They had a fleeting sense of Alfred beside them and then the field of their minds' view suddenly expanded, the wall of evil was pushed back to the edge of the cavern, and they could sense in the plinth itself great power that had been building up over thirteen centuries to the climax of Odric's awakening and that if that climax was halted there would be a big explosion in which they would all be killed. They could also see that the plinth had started a ten second countdown to the detonation – ten seconds of grace during which Odric could still be awoken – and two of those seconds had already gone.

Olly threw open the trunk and leapt out.

8... 7...

He raced round the edge of the cave towards the Commandos. They were under siege from Botwulf who was throwing green glass balls that exploded on impact like grenades. But the Commandos had already begun their dig towards the surface and were well protected.

As he ran Olly sent a polite but firm mental message to the Mole-Major.

Wait a moment, please, Sir. The Mole-Major paused. *We must replace the Stone. If we do not, an explosion will destroy us all. Please trust me. Once Odric has risen, we will try to take it again.*

6... 5...

The Mole-Major was accustomed to making split-second decisions. He had been hoping for contact from the children before now but supposed that without the Stone they had not been able to do it. Well, they were doing it now, even without the Stone. He recognised the significance and did a U-turn in the freshly dug tunnel.

4...

In less than a second he and the First Lieutenant were back out in the cave and running towards Olly.

Botwulf was astonished and enraged to see Olly appear. Then he saw the two mole officers break cover at high speed, the Stone swinging between them. He swore as he saw the moles reach Olly, who, like a relay racer, picked up the Stone and ran.

3...

'You shall not escape,' shrieked Botwulf, misinterpreting the boy's objective and with extraordinary speed covered the 15 metres that separated them. Olly was running for all he was worth towards the plinth, the Stone in his outstretched hand.

2...

When Botwulf landed on him from behind, he was less than two metres from his objective. They fell to the floor and momentum kept them sliding towards the plinth. But when they came to rest the Stone in Olly's outstretched hand was still one centimetre from its socket.

1…

With the weight of Botwulf on top him, Olly, face downwards, used all his strength to move himself forward. He flexed his ankles and pushed with his toes, at the same time stretching his arm forward as he had never stretched before…

Zero…

There! It was in. He twisted.

33

RISING

Aristotle and Ian had used back streets to reduce the chance of being seen but they need not have worried – the car park was deserted and the rescue helicopter, though locked, was unattended. Ian gnawed through rubber sealing strips at the corner of the door and, once inside, stripped insulation off two wires to the door switch. Shorting-circuiting them with a screwdriver opened the door wide enough for Aristotle to squeeze in and shut it again afterwards.

Ian remembered exactly how Liam had hot-wired the machine the previous week. In a few minutes he was sitting behind the windscreen ready to take off, his tablet lit up with a display of the helicopter's controls.

Aristotle, meanwhile, had found a downwards-facing window next to the external searchlight and strapped himself in beside it. Once airborne, they planned to head towards Whitby lighthouse and search for the top of the shaft.

'Ready?' shouted Ian, one paw poised over his touchscreen, the other grasping a tiny joystick connected to it.

'Yes,' called Aristotle, without conviction. He had never been in a helicopter, let alone a stolen one piloted by a mouse.

Ian, too, was nervous but excited as well. At least this was *doing* something, not just waiting around.

He started the engine and began to feel lift as the rotor got up to speed. The strong wind moved the helicopter sideways.

I'd better take off quickly, he thought, before we're blown into the Mobile Incident Room. He opened the throttle and the helicopter shot into the air, throwing him to the cockpit floor.

'Rats,' he muttered, frantically scrambling back up to the windscreen. By that time they were at two hundred feet, in cloud and being seriously buffeted by the wind.

He touched the *Hover* key while he tied himself in position. Then, grasping the joystick, he brought the helicopter slowly down until he could see whiteness from waves along the seashore. At that height the land, rising steeply behind the village, sheltered them from the worst of the weather but even so it was a bumpy ride. Glancing at the compass he turned the machine to follow the coast northwards and pressed the *Auto* key. The helicopter would now maintain course and speed on its own as they searched.

***

Bill Peterson woke up in a cold sweat and looked at his watch. Just after midnight. What a nightmare! He hadn't had one as bad as that since he was a child. He dreamed that the village was hit by an earthquake and fell into the sea. It was so realistic.

He knew it would be some time before he managed to sleep again so he got up in his dressing gown and went downstairs to make a cup of tea. On his way he looked out of the window of the children's empty bedroom, just to reassure himself that everything was normal. It was, except that the rescue helicopter was taking off from the car park.

Funny, he thought, as he put the kettle on.

***

In their trunk, Tilly and Liam were not sure what to do. Should they stay where they were in the hope they would not be detected, or should they jump out and try to help Olly? He was lying, winded, underneath Botwulf and the ground was once more starting to shake.

They made up their minds.

As they flung back the lid of the trunk, columns of smoke again shot out from the sides of the plinth, rapidly turning to fire. Olly and Botwulf, at the foot of the plinth, had to duck to avoid being burned. Tilly, with Liam in her pocket, ran towards them, keeping low, in the hope that the sisters would not see them. The sisters' attention, however, was either on their wounds or the arch of fire which was now re-forming over Odric. In the nick of time Olly had restarted Odric's awakening.

As the flames rose upwards, roaring and brightening at the same time, Botwulf sat up, still on Olly. To the children's surprise, he began to cackle with laughter. He had seen the joke. Odric awakened by his enemy the son of Alfred.

Tilly reached Botwulf and shoved at his shoulders with all her strength. He seemed hardly to notice her but the force of the push toppled him over on to his back, still laughing with rising hysteria. Released from the weight on top of him, Olly jumped up and the two children ran back to the side of the cave, to crouch behind their trunks.

Flames now shot down from the top of blazing arch to the supine body, dancing along it from head to foot. They were white-hot and Odric was incandescent beneath them.

He'll burn to ashes.

Odric was not burning to ashes. He was sighing and groaning with satisfaction, as though he was in a relaxing hot bath. His chest expanded as he seemed to take a deep breath of fire. For a moment the flames reduced in size as he drew them into his lungs then shot up again as he exhaled in a long ecstatic cry. This time the cry was not an inarticulate sound – it was a single triumphant word, easily heard over Botwulf's surreal laughter.

'Ali-i-i-ve.'

There was a sound of breaking chains, followed by a thunderclap and a blinding flash, which for a moment obliterated the watchers' view of the plinth. When the smoke began to clear, the flames had gone and a tall figure stood on the plinth, shrouded in black, head thrown back and arms outstretched in triumph.

The stinking monster was gone. Odric was risen.

34

SHOCK

At the pit the Colonel looked at his watch for the tenth time in as many minutes.

'Right,' he said. 'Midnight.'

He set off, Jess walking proudly beside him, Kiran and Daniel behind.

***

Smoke remnants curled around the sinister figure on the plinth. Botwulf, still cackling uncontrollably, managed to raise himself to his knees and regain some of his self-control.

'Welcome back, Master,' he said. 'The waiting is over. Your rise to power will be magnificent, and I shall continue to serve you as I have done over the long empty centuries.'

'You have done well,' said Odric, still standing on the plinth. 'Over the past centuries your words have occasionally found their way from my ears to my mind, so I have been aware of your efforts on my behalf. Now I am rejuvenated but you remain a spent relic and your smell is foul. Your usefulness is ended.'

The sisters tattled to themselves. If Botwulf's usefulness was ended, where did that leave them?

'Master,' protested Botwulf, 'do you not require my help in your endeavours? I alone of your former servants remain. There is no one else to do your bidding apart from me.'

'And us,' said the sisters.

Odric glanced at them briefly.

'And, Master,' Botwulf went on, 'I have further secrets to reveal to you.' Botwulf knew his Master well enough to have foreseen that he would be discarded unless he had something his master wanted. He was prepared.

'Speak,' said Odric, arms folded, disinterest in his voice.

'Master, you are rejuvenated now but as the years pass you will age as I have. The one who chained you thirteen centuries ago ensured I would remain alive to tend you but as you aptly observed I am a mere husk and will no doubt soon deteriorate and die.'

Who does he mean – the one who chained him? thought Olly and Tilly, their minds one.

'I have had many centuries to consider this problem,' Botwulf went on, 'and believe I have devised a way by which you and I can rejuvenate each other from time to time, using the Stone.'

'How do you know the process will work?' asked Odric sceptically. 'The Stone has been returned to you only recently.'

'I admit, Master, that it has not yet been tried but I have carried out tests which I think verify my theories. First we shall experiment on an unimportant subject,' his eyes flicked to the sisters and back, 'and if it is successful you may apply it to me. Then, in years to come I will apply it to you and so on.'

'Hmm,' said Odric quietly, his black eyes thoughtful. 'I have nothing to lose by your plan. We will begin shortly but first I will speak with Alfred's descendants.'

The children had been so absorbed in what was happening they had forgotten how exposed to danger they were.

Quick, run for it. They sprinted towards the door.

'Surely you do not wish to leave already,' said Odric, his words heavy with sarcasm. 'We have not even begun to get to know each other. Besides, I must thank you for raising me from my sleep.'

Botwulf cackled appreciatively as they reached the door and tried the concealed handle. It did not work.

'It's no use trying to escape.' he continued. 'Come forward so we can talk.'

Having no other option, the children turned and slowly walked towards the plinth.

He doesn't know we can communicate does he and he won't as long as we keep him out.

They had studied their mind maps and knew this for certain. Also, since Odric had awoken they had not needed to work so hard to keep the wall of evil out. It gave them a kind of confidence but they were still afraid.

Odric was a formidable sight – very tall and exuding dark strength. The hood of his cloak was back, revealing a pale complexion and terrifying black eyes.

'Let me look at you,' said Odric. The children felt as though he was looking right inside them. 'Ah yes, I see the family resemblance. What a shame Alfred himself is not here. I would have liked him to see you punished for his misdeeds.'

I am with you. Alfred's voice beside them, reassuring.

'For it is he who confined me so inconveniently,' Odric went on.

So that's why he wants us, Olly and Tilly realised.

'He and my foolish brother Edwin showed a weak characteristic that many humans share – compassion for their fellow beings. They sought to punish me with a long imprisonment that would cause me to change my character and become weak like them. Instead they played into my hands. Now I have returned and will be even stronger. The world will soon find out'

194

'You may not find that so easy,' said Olly boldly. 'The world has changed a lot in thirteen centuries. Now governments have powerful armies and weapons.'

Odric laughed. 'I will make governments bow down before me. Not only do I have the Stone but also the plinth. Alfred created it for his own purposes but with the Stone I will be able to harness its power for my own.'

What does that mean?

Alfred answered. *The plinth is a tool I made to magnify the effect of the Stone. For example to cure dozens of people of disease or injuries simultaneously rather than just one at a time. But like the Stone I cannot prevent its being used for evil so if Odric made a small explosion with the Stone, the plinth could make it a colossal one.*

This exchange took only an instant but there was much more the children wanted to know.

Later, said Alfred.

'The small Stone is useful and is all I had before,' Odric was saying, 'but now with the plinth I will have the power to cause earthquakes anywhere on earth. Explode whole cities in an instant. Cause entire armies to burst into flame. Bring about anything I want. I am impatient to begin but first I must attend to the small matter of eternal life. After that we will have a longer… chat.'

Olly and Tilly dared not think how that might turn out.

Botwulf handed Odric the Stone and whispered, 'Master, first you must experiment.' His eyes once more flicked to the sisters, who were standing, silent and sullen, a few metres away.

'Approach, sisters,' called Odric. 'Botwulf has told me of your help and I wish to reward you.'

The sisters were surprised and pleased. Botwulf had never rewarded them. They walked to the plinth and looked up at Odric, trusting and expectant.

'Here is your reward,' he said looking down at Astrid. Her wart trembled, its hair quivering in anticipation.

Odric held out the Stone with both hands and stared at her. Smiling, she raised one hand to take it. A spark crackled from it to her hand. She cried out and drew back as though she had been stung but a stream of sparks attached to her hand like a thread that she could not shake off. Her cry of pain became a prolonged scream as they spread all over her body.

The children watched in horror – Astrid was changing before their eyes. She was already old but in the space of a few moments her face became even more wrinkled and shrunken, her hair turned white and dropped out, her limbs became twisted and bent. Her scream became hoarse and stopped, her shrivelled throat unable to make a sound. She looked hundreds of years old and could no longer stand. She collapsed to the floor, a bag of bones.

Ingrid's squinting eyes bulged with fear.

'Hmm. Wrong direction,' said Odric, laughing loudly.

He tried again. This time sparks crackled towards both sisters. In just a few moments Astrid was back to normal but then both sisters began to change, this time getting younger instead of older. They became young women, then girls, then children, then babies, then…bats.

The sparking stopped and the two bats flew up into the air, circling round each other, until they disappeared into the darkness to seek out others of their kind.

'An amusing device,' Odric chuckled. 'Effective too, when properly controlled.'

'I thought it would not take you long to learn its secrets, Master,' he said ingratiatingly.

The children had not liked the Boyles but were appalled at the callous way Odric had treated them.

'So now,' continued Odric, holding out the Stone

towards Botwulf, 'I shall restore you to your prime, as I have been restored to mine.'

This time Odric controlled the process better but it took several minutes to undo thirteen centuries of decay. Afterwards, the bent creature was gone, along with the smell, and in its place was no longer a skin-covered skeleton but a muscular, erect figure, black cloaked like his master with long brown hair, sharp features and the characteristic hooked nose.

Botwulf laughed, his voice deeper but with the same jagged edge.

'So, Master, let your reign begin.'

35

THE PLINTH

In the rescue helicopter Ian wore a headset radio that patched him into the H.Q. system.

'H-hello H.Q.' he heard Dauntless Arvicola shout into his microphone, only just audible over the sound of crashing waves. 'N-nothing to report here, except the s-storm's getting worse.'

'Roger,' Ian chuckled, 'nothing new here either, except we've borrowed the helicopter and are heading towards you.'

A few minutes later an astonished Dauntless Arvicola, hanging by one arm out of the wheelhouse, saw them pass overhead. Heron's neck craned beside him.

'Wretched inelegant machines,' muttered Heron.

Jack was still asleep.

***

Odric and Botwulf were sitting at the table near the plinth. Odric was keen to hear Botwulf's briefing on the past thirteen centuries. They ignored the children, confident they could not escape.

What are we going to do now, the children asked each other,.

If the plinth is like the Stone, said Olly, *perhaps it can be used in a similar way. We haven't got the Stone to control it but we could try touching it.*

Alfred nodded. *I made the plinth in such a way that only a descendant of mine or someone with the Stone can use it. Your abilities strengthen in the face of evil and, as it is all around, you are very strong. I believe you will be able to control the plinth.*

Well the sooner we try it the better, said Tilly, *before Odric starts using it.*

It was between them and the place where Odric and Botwulf were sitting, so the children edged towards it, trying not to draw attention to themselves.

Since the countdown to Odric's rising part of their minds had continued to monitor the surrounding area and at that moment they noticed something.

Outside the door. Kiran, Daniel and the Colonel trying to get in. They started to feel hope again.

They concentrated for a moment and realised that their friends had tried the opening handle but found it locked as they themselves had

The Colonel must be on our side otherwise he'd know how to open it, they agreed.

Liam heard too. He had been keeping a very low profile and his knees had had a lot of exercise but through the children he had been aware of everything they had been aware of.

'Maybe I can help,' he said. 'The door machinery's got to be in that wall somewhere. Perhaps I can find it and unlock it.'

He did not wait for a reply. He was out of Tilly's pocket and down to the ground before you could say cat.

He was so scared he wanted to stop and wail with fright but he had acted without thinking and his legs were on automatic before he hit the floor. He just held his breath and ran.

As he reached the door, he saw the Mole-Major to his left beckoning vigourously. He changed course and quickly found himself in the entrance to a small tunnel. Most of the commandos were now well on their way to the village but the Mole-Major and his First Lieutenant had stayed behind to see what help they could give.

In Rabbit, Liam explained his mission and where

within the wall the door machinery was most likely to be. By fast exploratory digging the moles soon found it. Liam quickly delved inside amongst cog wheels and drive belts. In less than a minute he found the locking bar and pushed it aside. The Mole-Major was impressed.

Then he pointed to a metal rod running through the machinery. The ends disappeared into small holes in the rock, one leading to the outside and the other to the inside. 'At the ends of this are the handles that open the door,' he said. The three of them tried to turn it but were not strong enough.

Liam squeezed into the rod hole leading to the outside. He pulled himself forward hand over hand, determined to force his way through around the rod. He barely had room to breathe but after much effort, purple in the face and glasses steamed up, he broke though into the small cavity where the outside handle was. He pushed the hinged flap open to reveal the tunnel beyond, lit by the Colonel's torch.

Jess immediately noticed the movement and barked. The Colonel followed Jess's noseline and spotted Liam at once. The children and the Colonel were delighted to see him.

'He's a friend, you know,' Kiran told Liam authoritatively.

It took only a few moments talking to his tablet for Liam to introduce himself to the Colonel and to outline the situation.

'Right. Going in now,' said the Colonel. 'Stay well behind.'

Daniel put Liam into his pocket as the Colonel opened the door.

***

Crouching low behind the plinth, Olly and Tilly placed

their hands flat on its side and closed their eyes…

By now they were used to the sensation of using the Stone, of sharing each other's thoughts and so on. With the plinth it was different. They were awe-struck by its enormity. It felt as though they were inside a palatial echoing hall, bigger than the biggest cathedral they could think of.

Welcome, descendants of my creator. Their minds told them it was the voice of the plinth, deep and strong and trustworthy.

What is your command? it said. *I sense no injuries in you but there are some small creatures nearby who are hurt. Shall I repair them?*

He must mean the moles.

Yes, said Olly.

Executing, said the plinth.

Immediately three injured moles, being carried through newly dug tunnels, half way up to the village, stepped off their stretchers, smiled, yawned and resumed their customary positions in the platoon marching formation, to the astonishment and delight of their brothers-in-arms.

What is your next command? asked the plinth.

What now? The children thought. *Ask it to take Odric prisoner or kill him or something?*

Cannot comply, said the plinth evenly. *He holds the Stone.*

Obviously the plinth had read their thoughts. It now studied them in silence and they could tell it was becoming wary.

We'll leave you for the moment, said Olly and they both stopped touching the plinth.

We need to be careful. Let's study our minds to see if there's a way to stop the plinth reading them.

But they had no time. Odric and Botwulf had finished their conversation and were approaching the plinth.

A movement in the gloom near the door caught Olly's eye. Both Odric and Botwulf had their backs to it. Could it be help? Should they run or hold their ground?

'Nobody move,' – the Colonel shouting from the doorway, revolver at the ready.

Odric turned and assessed the situation in a flash. He closed his eyes, holding the Stone. He was connecting with the plinth. Then he opened them again and shouted to Botwulf.

'Deal with the intruders! We go to the castle.'

'But, Master… ' cried Botwulf desperately.

His master paid no attention. His eyes were closed again

The Colonel took careful aim at Odric. 'Drop that Stone and put your hands above your head.'

Take us to the castle, said Odric to the plinth with his mind.

Executing, said the plinth.

As the Colonel pulled the trigger, Botwulf threw a green glass ball to the ground and there was an intense flash that blinded the Colonel for several seconds.

Daniel, Liam and Kiran, coming in behind the Colonel, missed the flash by an instant and saw Odric disappear a microsecond before the Colonel's bullet reached him. It whistled harmlessly through the air where he had been standing and hit the wall on the other side of the cavern.

Botwulf rushed straight at Kiran and Daniel, shoving them aside as he ran out of the door.

It took Kiran, Daniel and Liam a moment to realise that Olly, Tilly and the plinth had also disappeared.

36

THE CASTLE

The storm intensified at midnight and hit the helicopter full blast as it rounded Lighthouse Point from where they could see Whitby Abbey ahead. The engine thundered and vibrated, struggling against the fierce elements. Reverting to manual, Ian found it increasingly difficult to control the bucking machine as they slowed to look for the shaft. He reduced height and the downward-pointing searchlight illuminated both the top of the cliff and, far below, waves crashing in quick succession against its foot.

'Wait, I think I've seen something,' shouted Aristotle, gripping his binoculars more tightly. 'Can you go a bit lower?'

Ian nodded grimly, concentrating on making a safe descent. The lower they came and the nearer to the cliff edge, the more capricious the wind became. Ferocious side winds one moment, lethal up or down draughts the next. At ten metres from the ground, he dared go no further.

'Yes, definitely something there,' Aristotle barked. 'Can you land?'

'Yes,' yelled Ian, not sure if he could.

***

As the Colonel's gun boomed, the plinth threw Olly and Tilly into a dark vortex where sight and sound ceased. Their stomachs turned over as though they were in free fall, tumbling over and over, then a few seconds later that sensation stopped and they were just floating comfortably in nothingness.

We are safe here for a short time, said Alfred.

Where are we? Both children felt to be in a dream-like state. Awake, but only just.

Slightly outside the normal world and time.

Like we're in another dimension or something? Olly asked.

You are on the way to Odric's castle in a place where time is elastic and can be stretched a little without changing the duration of your journey. It gives me a chance to explain some things to you. I know from your minds that you have many questions.

Alfred was right. Many questions and few answers.

When Botwulf created the Stone he had stumbled upon a great scientific discovery but was so intent on his narrow evil purposes that he was blind to its greater implications. In short he had found a way for humans to see into their own minds and use power they find there. Every mind is different and has different abilities many of which lie dormant unless they are awakened by learning or experience. The Stone offered a new way for everyone to reach their full potential.

Like it enabled us to look at our own minds and put Daniel's injuries right?

Exactly, but I quickly realised that in the wrong hands it could be used for great evil by the likes of Odric and Botwulf. That was why I restricted its users and kept the discovery secret.

According to Aristotle, said Olly, *after you and Edwin defeated Odric and Botwulf they were locked up in their laboratory. Why didn't you just leave them? They would have died eventually without being a threat to anyone.*

Of that I could not be sure. Botwulf had created the Stone. Perhaps he could create another to enable the two of them to escape or do something worse. I realised that somehow I would have to confront them and not wait too long before I did.

The children could see what he meant.

In a few months I became more proficient with the Stone and created the plinth – now is not the time to tell you how – which greatly extended what I could do. I was able to communicate with

Odric using it and tried to negotiate with him – the destruction of the Stone and any similar device in return for safe passage for the two of them to exile overseas. But he' would not listen. He was boastful and arrogant – nations would bow down before him and all that.

Using the plinth I could have killed both men without even going into the laboratory but Edwin would not hear of it and believed his brother could be redeemed. Out of compassion I agreed.

Instead I entered his mind and rendered him unconscious, making changes to his body that would keep him that way for thirteen centuries provided he was given nourishment. I also tried to alter his personality so that over time he would become less evil and perhaps repentant. But in that I was not successful. If anything he is worse than he was. In a way I am not surprised – I was young and overconfident and such alterations are difficult and delicate. I enabled Botwulf to live so he could look after his master and eventually be rejuvenated but I removed any ability he might have to make another Stone. Luckily in that I was successful.

Why thirteen centuries?

I felt it was a long enough period for human civilisation to develop ways of dealing with such men as Odric if he did not mend his ways. In my time a lot of the country is lawless and chaotic and men like Odric can flourish. I sense, however, that in your time civilisation has not progressed as far as I hoped.

My last step was to place Odric under the plinth's control because Edwin and I would naturally die after a normal lifespan and I built in a failsafe that the plinth would explode if anything prevented Odric's awakening, for I could not know that the Stone would be properly passed down the family.

No more now – your journey is ending...

In the next second a thunderclap with a flash of lightning welcomed the children back into reality and the howling heart of a storm.

They were standing with Odric on stone battlements at the top of a cliff, fierce wind and freezing rain beating against them. Across the bay the lights of a village twinkled dimly, barely visible through rain and sea spray. Looking down they saw a sheer drop to the bottom of the cliff where they could hear massive waves crashing against rock. In the far distance, beyond the village, were regular flashes from a lighthouse.

We're at Scar Point on the walls of the hotel garden – but we know there's no castle here.

More thunder and lightning. Odric swept them up, one under each arm and descended some steps on the landward side of the battlements. As the children struggled uselessly against his strength, a section of wall swung open and they entered. When it closed behind them Odric released the children and drove them in front of him down some more steps. At the bottom he threw open double doors.

'Welcome to my home. So good of you to pay a visit.' he mocked.

The large black-carpeted hall was draped with black wall hangings and was empty apart from the plinth in the centre, waiting for them. Several black chandeliers, festooned with lit candles, also black, hung from the vaulted ceiling.

All this, underground. How did no-one know that it was here?

Odric noted the children's puzzled expressions.

'So you were not told that my castle is down here?' he said, enjoying the moment. The children did not give him the satisfaction of a reply.

'Plinth, bind them,' said Odric harshly, holding out the Stone. Instantly, the children were bound hand and foot with black silk rope. They toppled over onto the carpet.

'So you thought to foil my plans by interfering with the plinth?' he continued.

The plinth must have told him we've been in, said Olly.

'Futile, of course, for I am far stronger than you. Pain will shortly teach you that lesson.'

Odric stalked off to the other side of the hall and hung up his wet cloak.

Oh dear, it's all gone wrong, said Tilly despondently. *How are we going to stop Odric now.*

We mustn't give up, said Olly. *What do we do, Alfred?*

Try accessing the plinth, even though you are not touching it. I believe the conditions are right.

But what then?

Let Odric know.

The children shut their eyes as they heard Odric returning and reached out to the plinth with their minds.

'Well I have you at last' he said with venom. 'Your interfering ancestor Alfred was foolish not to kill me when he had the chance because now I will make you pay for what he did to me.'

Welcome, descendants of my creator. Again the enormous echoing inside of the plinth.

Odric was disappointed not to have a response from the children. He liked people to quake in their shoes when he spoke. He looked more carefully at them. Eyes closed. Sleeping? No something else…

'Wretches,' he shouted as he realised what they were doing. He closed his eyes too.

Welcome Stone holder, said the plinth. *I await your command.*

Odric leered at the children across what seemed to be a deep chasm.

Expect no mercy from me, he said to them. *Plinth, suggest a few painful ways for these children to die and let them choose.*

37

SHAFTED

As the Colonel's eyes recovered from Botwulf's flash grenade, Kiran and Daniel were torn between pursuing Botwulf and racing round the cave for any clue as to where their friends and Odric had gone.

The Colonel was troubled at what Kiran and Daniel had seen.

'Devil take him. Castle means Scar Point. Must get there. Now. Tunnels too slow. Shaft only chance. Take me there.'

They ran out of the door, Jess in the lead. She presumed they were chasing Botwulf.

Meanwhisker had emerged from hiding and was at the top of the steps leading down to Botwulf's laboratory when Botwulf himself rushed through the doorway from the tunnel. She was surprised at the change in his appearance. She shrank back against the wall but he took no notice. He raced down the steps.

A few seconds later Jess bounded in followed by the Colonel. Meanwhisker saw Jess and froze. Jess's hair stood on end and then she accelerated, barking, her feet slipping on the rock. Meanwhisker turned tail and fled. She knew that Botwulf's room at the top of the steps was a dead end. Her only option was down the steps after Botwulf.

At the bottom she streaked across the cavern but was too late to get into the laboratory behind Botwulf, who slammed the rock door shut a second before she got there. She cowered, cornered.

Jess was in hot pursuit but as she passed the opening

into the shaft the Colonel, somewhat out of breath, called for her to wait. He had heard Botwulf running and the laboratory door shutting and did not want Jess in his line of fire if Botwulf came out again. Reluctantly, Jess obeyed.

'I'll get you later,' she barked in Rabbit across the cavern. Meanwhisker spat and showed her bottom.

The Colonel poked his head into the shaft, wrinkling his nose at the smell. He spotted the ladder of iron rungs. It would be a long, hard climb but he had no option. The sound of wind and thunder funnelled faintly down the shaft.

Kiran and Daniel caught up but stayed well back with Liam. They did not want any accidents this time.

***

When Wickfeather had called in at Section H.Q. for a short rest, he had been doubtful about Ian and Aristotle's plan to commandeer the helicopter but he understood their desire for action.

As the helicopter went northwards towards Whitby, he had flown southwards across the bay, towards Scar Point. The storm was worse. Thunder and lightning split the sky. The gale and torrential rain increased. He climbed, seeking less turbulent air, trying to use the wind rather than fight it.

By the time he reached a position directly over Scar Point he had seen nothing unusual so turned to head inland but as he did so there was a thunderclap and flash of lightning. For an instant it lit up three figures on the battlement walls surrounding the hotel garden. A tall one and two smaller ones, their bodies bent against the wind. He caught his breath. Surely, it could not be the two Peterson children? He descended for a closer look.

Flash. Lightning gave another instant of clarity. The

Peterson children were clearly recognisable, firmly held by a tall black-shrouded figure. It must be Odric. When the next flash of lightning came, the three figures had gone. He must report to Aristotle.

***

Dangerously strong gusts tossed the helicopter from side to side as Ian's paw hovered over the *Auto Land* key. If he hit it when they were beyond the cliff edge, the control system would land them in the sea. He could not see directly downwards so he turned the nose inland into the gale, reasoning that it would be safe to land when there was level ground on either side.

At full throttle the helicopter was only just making headway but was more stable. He was learning. He gave the engine all it had and inched forward over the land.

That should do it, he said to himself a few moments later, and pressed the key. The auto-pilot took over and in seconds they were down, wind still rocking them.

'Phew,' he said into his headset microphone for Aristotle's benefit, 'We're down but I think I'll leave flying to birds in future.'

Aristotle, looking slightly shaken, was waiting when Ian got to the starboard door.

'You'd better hang on to me,' said the badger. 'Otherwise you'll be blown away.'

Outside they had to shout to be heard above the howling wind. About twenty metres from the landing site were two large lumps of rock, like gateposts, not far from the edge of the cliff. The ground fell away sharply behind them.

'That's what I saw,' yelled Aristotle. 'It's almost as though they're markers.' They scrambled between them, hanging on to bushes and other vegetation, down to a small flat area a few metres below. Sure enough, the top of the shaft was there, concealed by undergrowth.

'What now?' asked Ian, although he already knew. It took only a short discussion to decide that he should go down. Aristotle did not admit it aloud but he knew that he himself was too old for such an enterprise.

The line and sling used for air-sea rescues hung from a pulley arm at the side of the helicopter. Ian released the winch lock and the line unrolled as the two of them pulled it to the top of the shaft. Ian was showing Aristotle how to operate the remote control for the winch when Heron arrived on an updraught, all feet and feathers, barely able to control his trajectory in the storm.

'Awkward graceless contraptions,' he said by way of greeting, referring to the helicopter. 'The miracle is that they fly at all.'

Aristotle and Ian smiled to themselves. They knew Heron of old. He was pleased to see them. So was Wickfeather who arrived almost at once.

'I thank heaven you are safe in these extreme conditions,' he said. 'Truly it is a strange night. When there is time you must tell me of your flight but first I must tell you what I have seen.'

Aristotle was worried by what he heard.

'Your news makes me fear the worst. Odric is risen and at large. With the Stone, I'll wager, and he holds the two children. They are clearly in great danger. We must go to Scar Point with whatever forces we can muster. You two birds should go now. Ian and I will follow when we can but first we must let Ian down the shaft. Even before your news we were concerned about those below. Now, who knows what destruction Odric will have left in his wake.'

'Right,' said Heron and leapt into the air, feet narrowly missing Aristotle as the wind caught him.

Wickfeather managed a more orderly take-off.

Ian handed Aristotle a small handheld radio and stepped onto the sling.

'If you stay near the top of the shaft, we can talk to one another by radio,' he said. Ian was still wearing a headset. He tied himself to the sling with a few strands of rope he gnawed loose. Aristotle started the winch and Ian's descent began.

Down and down he went in the fetid air, thinking about Jack's amazing flight up the shaft and also about how far down the bottom might be. Occasionally, he looked up but the top soon disappeared in the darkness. At first, he and Aristotle could hear each other shout but gradually the sound became muffled, then inaudible. Fortunately the radios worked well.

I hope this rope's long enough, thought Ian

**

Botwulf, energised by his rejuvenation, moved purposefully round his laboratory selecting a few items essential for his escape. He was furious with his master for leaving him behind. It would have been so easy to order the plinth to take the four of them to the castle, or even just the two of them. After all, the children were expendable. True, they had somehow accessed the plinth, but if they were dead they would not be able to do so. Obviously, his master had yet to be convinced of the value of his faithful servant. Well, he would go to the castle anyway. He knew he could leap over the pit and easily outrun pursuers.

When he was ready, he opened the door a crack and threw out a glass grenade.

The children and the Colonel were out of range on the other side of the cavern but thick smoke billowed towards them.

Taking advantage of it, Botwulf ran out of the laboratory towards the steps. Meanwhisker seized the moment and followed at his heels, almost invisible behind his cloak.

The Colonel saw Botwulf racing out of the gloom and blocked his path, tensing for a collision.

Botwulf nimbly sidestepped, caught the Colonel a glancing blow with his elbow and was on the stairs before anyone knew what was happening.

Meanwhisker was left exposed only a couple of metres from Jess, who flung herself on the cat.

Immediately they seemed to fuse into a single entity, biting, spitting, growling and rolling over and over as they fought. Meanwhisker was smaller and more agile but Jess had superior strength and bigger jaws.

In less than a minute Meanwhisker was badly wounded and bleeding at the back of the neck. She had to get away. Using an old cat's trick she suddenly went limp, which made Jess relax her grip. At once, Meanwhisker pulled free. Refuge, she needed refuge. Gathering her remaining strength she jumped onto the sill of the dark opening into the shaft.

As Jess braced herself to follow there was a movement in the shaft at the top of the opening. Feet first, Ian and the sling appeared, descending rapidly in the shadows behind Meanwhisker.

'Heel,' said the Colonel but Jess was already in mid flight at Meanwhisker, jaws open. Meanwhisker, desperate for a way out, turned and saw the rope behind her. Deliverance. She lunged for it but Ian realised what was happening. By now below the opening, he kicked himself away from the wall with all his strength, swinging like a pendulum towards the far side of the shaft. Too late Meanwhisker saw the rope go out of reach. Already falling, she tried to flip round in mid air, her front paws connecting with the sill. But there was nothing to grip.

Her claws scraped white grooves in the rock as she slid back into the abyss. A long scream of fear continued until its ever decreasing echoes were lost in the deep.

Kiran, Daniel and Liam shuddered. Jess barked triumphantly. The Colonel stepped forward, grabbed the still descending rope and pulled Ian back up.

'Good show,' he said, stroking Ian's back.

38

LIAM

Dauntless Arvicola and Jack heard Heron's voice on the wind even before he came into view.

'Change course for Scar Point, Captain,' he was shouting as he landed with a bump on the heaving deck.

Dauntless Arvicola swung the wheel. As the slim craft surged forward, Heron told them what Wickfeather had seen. With the wind behind her and the engines at full throttle, *S.S. Dauntless* had never moved so fast.

***

The Colonel told Kiran and Daniel to go back up to the village.

'You can't leave us here,' said Kiran indignantly.

'We want to go to Scar Point, too,' said Daniel.

'No time,' said the Colonel. 'Must use the shaft. Then helicopter. Urgent. Olly and Tilly. Grave danger. Duty calls. Take this.'

He pulled a second revolver out of his backpack.

Daniel's eyes widened as he reached for it but Kiran was ahead of him.

'*I'll* take charge of that,' she said, seizing it.

The Colonel showed them the safety catch and how to hold the gun at arm's length when firing.

'Just in case,' he said.

Then he patted Jess on the head, secured the sling round his chest and climbed into the shaft.

'Ok, haul us up,' said Ian into his headset from the Colonel's top pocket. Aristotle activated the winch.

Liam could have gone with the Colonel too but said he'd stay behind to see that the children were alright. He opted for Daniel's pocket again. Kiran, Daniel and Jess were soon climbing the steps on the first leg of the long walk home.

***

As Botwulf reached the main tunnel, he paused. Why was he running from the intruders? They would continue to be an annoyance unless eliminated. Returning to the steps, he sidled half way down and cursed silently as he saw the Colonel disappearing out of reach up the shaft. But a slow, twisted leer spread across his face when the two children and the dog started walking towards where he crouched.

***

Emerging from the top of the shaft, the Colonel took off the sling, shook Aristotle's hand and smiled grimly.

'Good work,' he shouted, his words almost lost in the roaring storm. Ian had to hang on tight as he climbed to the ground to translate for Aristotle and explain the Colonel's plan

'Let's go,' the Colonel added, striding towards the helicopter. The two animals hurried after him, the gale pinning Ian's whiskers to his cheeks.

The Colonel settled into the pilot's seat and started the engine. Aristotle and Ian hastily strapped themselves into the navigator's seat beside him. There was obviously no need for Ian to fly the helicopter this time. The Colonel was flicking switches and preparing for takeoff as though he did it every day. There was a new intensity and determination about him.

'Hold on,' he shouted and the helicopter leapt into the turbulent sky.

***

Daniel, Kiran, Liam and Jess were wary as they entered the main tunnel and turned left towards the village.

Botwulf was probably a long way ahead of them by now, or half way to Scar Point by some secret route known only to him but they did not want to take chances. Kiran held the revolver and Daniel walked enviously beside her, lighting their way with the torch. Jess was in front. All four badly wanted to get to Scar Point to help Tilly and Olly.

At the pit the Colonel's temporary bridge was still in place. Kiran stepped forward and tested it with her foot. It seemed sound enough but rather narrow.

'Come on, Daniel,' she said over her shoulder.

'He will move when I say,' grated an all too familiar voice.

Kiran spun round, horrified. Botwulf held Daniel from behind, a silver knife at his throat. Daniel could feel the point of the blade against his skin. He dare not move a muscle. He still clutched the torch, his arm rigid with fright.

Curwald snarled at the bottom of the pit. He had picked up the scent both of his erstwhile prey and the master he loved and loathed. Perhaps at last he was to be fed. His spirits rose.

'Drop the knife,' said Kiran, raising the revolver and slipping off the safety catch. She tried to sound determined but a tremor in her voice betrayed her fear.

'If you are sure you will hit me and not your brother, please fire now,' said Botwulf, his voice jarring like a rusty gate.

Taking careful aim, Kiran tightened her finger on the trigger. Liam, peeping out of Daniel's pocket, put his paws over his eyes.

After what seemed like an age Kiran relaxed and lowered the gun. It was just too risky.

Liam breathed again. Botwulf smirked. The softness of these people was so predictable. In the same position, he would not have hesitated to pull the trigger.

'Throw your gun into the pit,' Botwulf ordered.

Kiran complied. Curwald pounced hopefully on the weapon then yowled at yet another disappointment.

Jess growled but Kiran held her firmly. She did not want to risk the knife slipping. Botwulf ordered girl and dog to lie face down on the floor. 'Remain where you are for fifteen minutes,' he ordered.

Then, still holding Daniel in front of him, he advanced onto the bridge. The torch shone downwards from Daniel's hand, lighting the beast below. As they began to cross Daniel felt a movement in his pocket. Liam! He had almost forgotten him but what use was a mouse in this situation? He just hoped he would lie low and not get hurt.

Liam was not lying low. Taking care to keep out of Botwulf's sight, he climbed up to Daniel's collar, dangerously close to the knife. They were half way across the bridge.

Down in the pit Curwald looked up expectantly, salivating at the thought of Daniel, his tasty morsel.

Botwulf was enjoying himself. He would soon be away up the tunnel to join his master but there was no need to hurry. When he reached the other side of the pit it would be easy to push Daniel into it. After all, he did have some obligation to Curwald. In the confusion, he would toss a glass grenade across to the other side to dispose of that irritating girl.

Daniel felt Liam's movements. I'd better be ready for anything, he thought.

Without stopping to think whether or not he was frightened, Liam ran round Daniel's collar and launched Ian's catpin at Botwulf's face.

Botwulf shrieked, let go of Daniel and dropped the knife.

Daniel was not sure what had happened but did not stay to find out. He ran across the bridge to the other side. Liam hung on to Daniel's collar shouting 'Run, Run,' in mouse at the top of his voice.

Botwulf did not pursue them. The catpin was protruding from his right eyelid, pinning it to the eyeball. Every time he tried to blink he felt excruciating pain. He clawed the air with one hand whilst steeling himself to pull out the catpin with the other, but every time he touched it he screeched in agony.

Blindly he took a step forward and missed his footing, swayed, almost righted himself then took another step to regain his balance. This time he stepped into thin air. With a cry of surprise and fear he toppled into the pit.

His cry became a scream as Curwald threw himself at his master. All Curwald's pent-up resentment at Botwulf's tyranny over hundreds of years erupted in bloodlust such as he had never felt before. The joy of teeth tearing flesh, of fresh blood. His master had given him the greatest gift of all – himself.

His master had also given him several other gifts. When Curwald's teeth penetrated one of the glass grenades concealed in Botwulf's cloak, an explosion atomised the bodies of both beings, creating a bloody mist that hung in the air for several seconds before slowly spattering to the ground.

39

CONFLICT

After Odric's command to the plinth to create death plans for Olly and Tilly there was a pause. Then,

Executing.

Immediately there appeared before the children's eyes, like the pages of a book hanging in the air one behind the other, about a dozen different death plans ranging from simple like being thrown from battlements to more complicated like being transported to a distant part of the world to be dropped into a volcano.

Odric smiled in satisfaction. *Excellent, plinth. Very creative. Now, daughter of Alfred, tell me how you would like to die.*

Both she and Olly heard Alfred's voice in their ears.

Make no choice. It will destroy you if you do.

I will not choose. she said, and summoning courage she did not feel, added, *If you try to kill us we will find a way to kill you.* Olly agreed out loud.

Odric found this funny. *And exactly how do you propose to do that?* He sneered. *You are bound hand and foot and I have control of the plinth – the most powerful weapon in the world.*

We're warning you, Olly sent to him boldly, somehow drawing strength from the presence of Alfred.

Oh I am really frightened now, Odric jeered. *But I will take my chances and choose your ends for you. Let me see… Ah yes here's good one – being bitten to death by giant rats. You first, daughter of Alfred. You brother and I will derive amusement from watching you die. Plinth, apply that plan to her.* The children felt strangely detached yet very frightened at the same time.

Again the plinth paused.

Regrettably, honoured Stone carrier, and with great respect, I cannot execute.

What? shouted Odric. *Do I not carry the Stone? Have I not the right to command you?*

Yes, Sir. And if the descendants of my creator had chosen to die I could have done what you ask. The plinth sounded apologetic.

Odric's response was ice cool. *If I command you to kill these children, you will comply.*

Sir, please do not do so. I cannot tell what the consequences will be.

Again, I will take my chances, laughed Odric, adding loudly and distinctly, *Plinth kill these children. That is an order.*

Pause.

A wall of fire erupted from the chasm separating Odric from the children and the plinth gave a wail of anguish.

Command conflict, it shrieked. *Attempting to resolve… Command conflict. Attempting to resolve… Command conflict. Attempting to resolve…*

Opening their eyes to the real world, the children saw the plinth begin to throb and grow red hot. They sensed that not only was its brain in a loop but also tremendous energy was building up inside that at any moment would result in a self-destructive explosion.

Let us combine our minds against this new danger, said Alfred.

In the last second before the explosion their minds joined to create an invisible barrier above and below the plinth and round three of its four sides.

It exploded with colossal force, instantaneously feeding and strengthening the barrier, which reacted to bind tighter.

The plinth blew apart into tiny fragments that were blown as though from a cannon in the only free direction, through the wall at the far end of the hall creating a gaping hole, beyond which there was only darkness, wind and lashing rain.

Phew, the children said to each other, relieved.

Odric emerged from behind a pillar holding the Stone.

You may have destroyed the plinth, he snarled, *but I still have the Stone. I said that you would die and now you shall.*

***

Low over the sea, the Colonel slowed the helicopter to walking pace and carefully surveyed the Scar Point cliffs. He knew the castle was below ground and hoped the face of the cliff held clues to the entrance but it was featureless apart from rocky outcrops and a few bushes.

Suddenly, rock and debris exploded outwards from the cliff, leaving a large hole. A flash of lightning momentarily lit up a dark hall beyond.

The Colonel's eyes glinted steely grey as he pulled back the stick into a climb and landed on the cliff above.

'Suggest you stay here,' he shouted to Ian and Aristotle as he unstrapped himself. 'Monitor radio.' He tapped a handheld transceiver clipped to his belt.

Sliding open a side door, he jumped to the ground and fought his way against the foul weather to the edge of the cliff. Without pausing he began to climb down. It was perilously steep and he had no rope but despite his age he was sinewy and agile. Using every possible nook and cranny in the wet rock he scrambled and slithered his way towards the top of the jagged opening below.

Back in the helicopter, Aristotle was worried.

'The danger is immense, Ian. There must be something we can do to help.'

Ian did not reply. He was no longer in the helicopter.

40

COMBAT

Odric towered over Olly and Tilly holding the Stone in both hands. His coal-black eyes glared down at them, bigger and colder than they had ever been.

This is how you will die, Odric chortled, holding the Stone out towards the void at the end of the hall.

Wooden roof beams were lying on a pile of rubble, lashed by rain. As the children watched, a sheet of fire shot up from them.

And you will die alone, he added.

What shall we do, Alfr... the children were asking – but were cut off from each other in mid thought.

'Oh!' Tilly could not stop herself exclaiming unhappily.

Odric leered at her. 'As I suspected – you were communicating – but now I have prevented it.'

It was worse than that – they could no longer feel Alfred's presence or use any mental powers at all.

'See,' Odric laughed, pointing to the blazing beams. 'You will burn brighter than the wood but when you have burned a little, I shall stop the flames with boiling water, like this...' a steaming cascade fell upon the flames, dousing them. '...to prolong your life – and your agony. When I am ready, I will re-ignite the flames but only for a little while, for your screams will be delicious to me.'

He smiled as the children looked at the curtain of steam in horror.

'Now your time has come,' he shouted triumphantly, holding the Stone out towards them.

The children braced themselves and closed their eyes.

'No, *your* time has come, Odric,' shouted a familiar voice.

They opened their eyes to see the Colonel burst through the steam behind Odric, revolver in hand. Odric had no time to react. The Colonel fired twice, hitting Odric each time.

He staggered several steps towards the children, clutching his chest and grimacing in pain, then fell face down and was still.

'Cut that a bit fine,' said the Colonel mildly.

The children could not believe it. He cut them free and briefly explained how he came to be there.

'Where's the Stone?' asked Olly. 'We must find it.'

They began to search the floor around Odric.

A burst of noise came from the Colonel's radio. He unclipped it from his belt and walked back towards the opening to improve reception.

'Calling Ian, calling Ian,' said Aristotle in Rabbit. 'Where are you? Come in please.'

Neither the Colonel nor the children understood but they recognised Aristotle's voice.

'He must want to know what's happening,' said Olly looking up. 'Let's tell him. Ian'll translate.'

The children suspended their search for the Stone and hurried to where the Colonel stood.

'The Colonel's saved us,' said Tilly into the radio. 'Odric's dead.'

'Not quite,' said a triumphant voice.

They turned in horror to see Odric standing once more, with the Stone in his hand. He smiled darkly, enjoying the surprise on their faces.

'Even as I fell,' he crowed, 'I did not lose my presence of mind. I sensed the Stone beneath me and healed myself.'

'Damn you,' said the Colonel, fumbling to draw his revolver.

Odric held out the Stone and the Colonel's revolver flew into the air, firing two shots as it went. They ricocheted past the children but one hit the Colonel in the shoulder.

'Damn you again,' shouted the Colonel and ran at Odric, catching him off balance.

They wrestled. The Colonel, despite his shoulder, hit Odric again and again with his fists. Odric hit back with the Stone, raining blows on the Colonel's head. They fell to the ground, rolling over and over as the Colonel tried to grasp the hand in which Odric held the Stone.

The children froze for a moment then joined in. They each grabbed one of Odric's arms. Olly tried to prise open Odric's fingers to release the Stone but could not move them. The Stone was adding to Odric's strength and he tossed the children aside with ease. The Colonel continued to fight furiously, seemingly oblivious to his wound but he could not indefinitely withstand Odric's superior size and strength. Suddenly, Odric threw him off and he fell motionless against the wall.

Odric stood up, framed in the gap left by the explosion, wind blowing his robe. 'Prepare to burn,' he snarled looking straight at the children.

They turned to run but heard a roar as the Colonel, once more on his feet, half loped, half staggered forward and launched himself through the air at Odric.

'Yaaahhhh,' he bellowed as his good shoulder hit Odric in the midriff, propelling them both through the opening in the cliff face and into the stormy darkness beyond.

The children rushed to the edge and looked down but could see only luminescent surf below. Then, ahead of them, four or five metres from the edge, they saw both men, not falling but tumbling over and over in mid-air as they fought. Odric still clutched the Stone, using it to hold them up, the Colonel again trying to take it from him.

'Revolver,' bellowed the Colonel. 'One shot left.'

'OK,' Tilly called, while Olly ran back to look for it. He returned almost at once.

'Got it,' he yelled.

He took careful aim but hesitated. The two were twisting and turning as they fought. He might hit the Colonel.

'Fire now,' the Colonel shouted and let go of Odric.

'Queen and countryyy,' he yelled as he fell into blackness.

Tilly screamed and Olly's trigger finger jerked, almost as a reflex. He hit Odric in the neck. Odric grimaced with pain but held onto the Stone.

'He'll use it to heal himself,' Tilly shouted.

Odric, still hovering, raised his head and gazed straight at the children, but his eyes were vacant as he focussed inwards on his injuries.

A large white bird with black wingtips appeared, dive bombing Odric's head in an attempt to distract him. Wickfeather! Then a large grey bird joined in. Heron!

Suddenly, the children saw a movement on Odric's arm. Surely it could not be but, yes, it was. A mouse. Ian!

Oblivious to danger, he raced down Odric's sleeve, heading for the Stone. In two seconds he was there. The children saw his mouth open and a flash of lightning illuminated his front teeth as he sank them into the soft underneath of Odric's wrist.

Odric cried out in pain and let go of the Stone.

'Ian,' shrieked Tilly as he and Odric plummeted two hundred metres to the bottom of the cliff.

Wickfeather dived after Ian but could not catch him.

Heron, caught the Stone in his beak and swooped up to drop it into Olly's hand. There was no time for words. Tilly slapped her hand on it too. At once they understood and dismantled the blockages that Odric had created.

Looking down, their vision enhanced by the Stone, they saw Odric had landed among seething waves near the water line, badly injured yet still alive. Painfully he clawed and crawled his way out of the sea onto the rocky shore. For a second the children felt Alfred behind them and then a lightning strike with a simultaneous thunderclap blasted a huge boulder out from the face of the cliff. Odric looked up, holding out his arm as though to shield himself but the boulder fell directly onto him, crushing out the remaining life.

The boulder bounced on and in the instant before it hit the heaving sea, the children saw a small boat directly in its path. It was too late to do anything. They waited in horror for *S.S. Dauntless* to be smashed to matchwood. The crash of the boulder hitting the water could be heard at the top of the cliff and concentric shockwaves of water leaped upwards and outwards.

Incredibly, on the crest of the largest wave, they saw the ship, engines racing, heading out from the centre of the maelstrom – and hanging over the stern rail was Jack, hauling in a bedraggled but obviously living mouse.

'Bad night for a swim,' said Jack, as he threw a blanket over Ian.

41

THE COLONEL

The Colonel lay on a ledge a few metres above the sea, horribly injured.

We must retrieve him, said Alfred, back with them

By the power of their minds they carefully raised him back up to the castle and laid him gently on the floor of the hall. They used Olly's jacket as a pillow.

The Colonel was unconscious and his breath came in groans. In addition to the bullet wound in his shoulder, every other part of his body seemed to be broken or bleeding. Now and then his eyelids fluttered and his lips moved as though he was trying to say something.

We must try to help him, said the children.

He may be beyond help, said Alfred sadly.

Holding the Stone, they gently touched the Colonel's temples and closed their eyes.

The river was fast flowing and deep this time. The Colonel was lying on the opposite bank, eyes closed.

Colonel, they shouted but he could not hear them above the sound of the water racing past.

I'll cross, said Olly.

He waded into the water to chest level, then swam. Although he was a strong swimmer, he only just made it to the other side. The Colonel had moved further away from the bank.

Olly, his mind one with Tilly and Alfred, knelt and put his hands on the Colonel's shoulders to look at his injuries. They were so extensive he did not know where to begin.

The Colonel opened his eyes and spoke.

Ah, Olly. Hoped you'd come. Heard the shot. Did you get him?

Yes, said Olly, *but he started to heal himself so Ian stepped in.*

He told the Colonel what had happened and of Ian's courage.

Cracking good mouse, said the Colonel smiling. *Sneaked into my pocket. Didn't realise. Odric really gone?*

Yes, said the children.

Well done, said the Colonel, *Team effort. Privilege to serve with you.*

They could tell he was getting weaker. All the time he and Olly were moving further away from the river and in the distance ahead they could see a pinpoint of light that was getting larger.

Family honour satisfied. Known for years this was coming.

How do you mean? asked Olly.

Edwin and Odric were my ancestors, said the Colonel. *Edwin tried to be fair to his brother. Mistake. Bad lot. Should have been killed. Family realised soon after. Pledged to serve and protect the Crown until things put right. Thirteen centuries later – down to me. Family archives required it.*

The Colonel was very weak now and the children wanted to help him

Let's get started, said Tilly.

The Colonel smiled faintly.

No.

But we must try, the children pleaded.

End of road. Done my bit. No need to carry on. Had my life.

He is right, said Alfred. *Everyone reaches their time. The Stone can only help if there is a strong will to live.*

The pinpoint of light was the size of a tennis ball and growing. Olly felt a warm glow radiating from it.

Go back now, said the Colonel, sounding weaker but smiling again. *Not right for you to leave the world. Lots for you*

to do. Remember me when you can. Been a pleasure knowing you.

Same here, said the children with tears in their eyes. *We owe you our lives.* The tennis ball had doubled in size.

Please look after Jess, said the Colonel, his voice barely a whisper and his eyes closing.

We will, we will, said the children, weeping.

As they watched, a peaceful expression transformed the Colonel's face and he floated away towards the light.

Once Olly was back to the safe side of the river the children opened their eyes and as they looked down at the Colonel's lifeless body they once more became aware of the outside world. The storm had passed, the wind had dropped and dawn was already brightening the sky.

At the bottom of the cliff, Odric's body had disappeared, swept away in the backwash of the boulder that killed him.

They climbed the steps from the castle hall and swung open the stone door leading to the battlements. A solemn Aristotle was there to meet them, with Wickfeather.

The Colonel was a very brave man, said Aristotle.

You know then, said Tilly dully.

We heard everything, said Wickfeather, *your minds broadcast it to us all.*

The children had no idea.

Come, said Aristotle. *It is time to rest.*

The children realised they were exhausted but they needed to speak to Alfred again.

Later, he said.

Heron arrived, a little more sedately now the wind had dropped. Lashed to his back and slightly shaken but otherwise in good spirits was Ian, just picked up from *S.S. Dauntless* and none the worse for his dramatic fall and soaking.

'That's a first,' he said as he untied himself and

climbed down. 'Thought you might need some help getting back to the village.'

Heron asked Tilly to smooth down the feathers where Ian had been sitting.

They reverently lifted the Colonel's body into the helicopter and, with Ian at the controls, took off across the bay.

Halfway across they saw below them *S.S. Dauntless* steaming confidently in the same direction. A flagpole had been lashed to the wheelhouse and a M.I.C.E. flag flew at half-mast.

'Look,' said Tilly, tears in her eyes, 'in honour of the Colonel.'

In the soft light of dawn, they saw Dauntless Arvicola and Jack stand to attention and salute the flag.

As the helicopter descended to the car park, Kiran, Daniel and Liam were there waving, Jess beside them, all safely back from the tunnels. They had come up through the Boyles' shop to avoid the questions from Mr and Mrs Akram that would have arisen if they had appeared in Daniel's' bedroom.

They clambered in to be reunited with their friends. It was still too early for anyone else to be about. The Mobile Incident Room was locked and deserted.

Jess howled with grief when she saw the Colonel's body, for she had been with him since she was a puppy. Olly and Tilly stroked and hugged her, spoke of the Colonel's heroism and bravery and told her that his last thought had been for her.

Daniel and Kiran were amazed at what they heard. Then it was the turn of Olly and Tilly to be amazed as the Akrams described the end of Botwulf and Curwald.

Aristotle raised a serious point.

'You children will need to explain about the Colonel to the police,' he said.

They all knew the truth would not be believed but there was no time to discuss what to say. A red faced policeman ran heavily across the car park towards them. He had heard the helicopter come in.

Aristotle hid behind the winch. Ian dived into Olly's pocket and Liam into Kiran's.

'Now then,' said the policeman, poking his head through the door, 'what's going on here?'

When he saw four grimy, unkempt children, a dog and the Colonel's body he gaped and made a call on his radio. Within a few minutes the Inspector arrived.

'This is my brother who was lost,' said Kiran pointing to Daniel, who was heading towards the cockpit for a look around. On the spur of the moment she told him that she, Olly and Tilly had gone to look for Daniel on their own, had got into difficulties and the Colonel had come to rescue them in the helicopter. It was broadly true.

'How did he die?' asked the Inspector.

Olly had an inspiration. 'There was a big cliff fall at Scar Point in the storm,' he said.

'So he was caught in it,' said the Inspector, making an assumption that Olly hoped he would. 'You had a lucky escape but how did you get the helicopter back here.'

'That's down to me,' came a voice from the pilot's seat.

Daniel, telling a whopper.

'You mean you piloted it?' asked the Inspector, incredulous.

'Well, I've seen it often enough on TV,' he said.

The other children were speechless. In their pockets Ian and Liam rolled about laughing.

While they had been talking more police had arrived as well as news media. Soon cameras were rolling and reporters were demanding to speak to Daniel. He told them he had been for a walk late at night and fallen down a hole. A travesty of the truth, but they were more interested in the helicopter flight.

Soon Mr and Mrs Akram appeared, to find Daniel giving a live interview on local TV news. Mrs Akram burst into the picture, overjoyed to see her son. All over the region people saw her hugging him and weeping over the tragic yet heroic death of the Colonel.

'Can we go now?' Olly asked the Inspector as the interviewer signed off.

'You certainly can,' he said. 'After what you've been through you need some rest. I'll see to the formalities.'

A black hearse was drawing up beside the helicopter to take the Colonel's body to a Chapel of Rest.

Aristotle and the two mice managed to slip away in all the confusion. Aristotle sent an email as soon as he arrived at Section H.Q.

The grandparents had already heard what had happened when Olly, Tilly and Jess got back to the cottage. Grandpa was on the phone to their mother.

'Yes, the police say they're fine. Ah, here they are now, just walking in the door. A bit tired perhaps. No, we thought they were at the Akrams but apparently they had an idea of where Daniel might be and decided to investigate for themselves. Quite brave really.'

Grandpa winked at them and listened to the telephone for a moment. They could hear their mother laying down the law. 'Yes, yes, I know. I'll certainly tell them they shouldn't go out without someone knowing where they're going.' Pause. 'Well, the weather wasn't too good, raining a bit, but they were well wrapped up.' He rolled his eyes to the ceiling and the children grinned. 'Yes, all's well that ends well and they're pretty much heroes over here. Now, how's the decorating going?'

The conversation went on for some time after that,

mainly about painting the kitchen, but the children did not listen. They turned their attention to the breakfast Granny was putting on the table. Luckily she was able to beg a can of dog food from a neighbour so Jess had a good meal too but she ate dejectedly and her tail hardly wagged at all. After that the children drifted upstairs to their room in a trance of tiredness. Olly put the Stone between them on the bedside table.

I will take my leave of you, said Alfred, appearing in the children's minds.

But where are you going?

I will be where I have always been – in my own home in my own time. Using the Stone, I found I could see across time to connect with it in the future when it is used by a descendant.

The children struggled to understand.

So the three of us are using the same Stone but in different times?

Yes, the Stone responds to the power our minds develop when we face a threat of evil. The greater the evil the more powerfully our minds respond so the easier it is for the Stone to keep us in touch with each other. You two have responded with remarkable power. It proves the Peterson blood remains strong.

Amazing, they thought, trying hard to grasp what it all meant.

What now though? Will we see you again? Tilly asked.

That I cannot tell – perhaps, if you face a big enough threat to the safety of animals or people. It has been a privilege to meet you but for obvious reasons I hope that you do not face such danger again in your lifetime. Your M.I.C.E. friends will understand that.

Saddened at the parting the children were silent, thinking how much they had relied on Alfred and grown to respect him.

He read their minds and smiled warmly.

Farewell, he said.

Bye – and thank you for helping us, the children said.

The children were soon asleep, too tired even to think over what Alfred had said.

Downstairs Grandpa had lit the fire and Jess slept in front of it. He stroked her from time to time, especially when she made wuffling noises and her paws tried to run as she relived dramatic scenes in her dreams.

***

The children were awoken in the afternoon by tapping at the bedroom window. Heron, in message mode. They had to touch the Stone to understand him.

'Meeting, Section H.Q. Tomorrow morning, eleven o'clock. Please tell the Akrams. Bye.' He flew away before the children could speak a word.

'We can't stay for it,' said Olly. 'It's Monday tomorrow. We'll have to go home tonight to be at school in the morning.'

They ran down to the Akrams with Jess to give Heron's message to Kiran and Daniel and to say goodbye. Daniel opened the door wreathed in smiles to tell them his Dad had phoned the head teacher of Olly and Tilly's school, a friend from his college days. She had seen the TV coverage and had readily agreed that the Peterson children needed a couple of days off school to get over their experience. Naturally, Mr Akram allowed Kiran and Daniel the same.

Kiran and Daniel stroked and hugged Jess, for she was still a very sad dog.

Before it was dark Grandpa took Jess for a long walk along the cliff top and back along the beach. The fresh air, exercise and nice smells made Jess feel a bit better.

Later, Olly and Tilly realised that although they were still telepathic between themselves, it was only when they touched the Stone. And they were unable to examine their own minds, or see the surrounding area, or any of the things they had become used to.

It must be because the evil has gone. Alfred said our powers grew when the evil got stronger.

The boulder that killed Odric, said Tilly. *Did it fall by accident or did Alfred cause the lightning, or was it us making it happen without realising?*

I was wondering that too.

42

HONOURS

By Monday morning the village was back to normal. The police, the helicopter and the Mobile Incident Room had gone. The newspaper boards said:

HELI–BOY! – DARING DAWN FLIGHT

No one saw the four children and Jess enter Section H.Q. All their M.I.C.E. friends were there and all of them in one way or another came up to Jess and said how sorry they were about the Colonel and what a brave man he was. It made Jess feel better and quite proud.

Aristotle called them all into the conference room for the meeting. Nurse Elaine and Ian sat together, smiling, talking and holding hands.

Aristotle made a speech describing in detail the part each one of them had played in the whole affair. The mice came in for special mention as did Dauntless Arvicola and Jess, and there was loud cheering when Liam interrupted to give an eye-witness account of Meanwhisker's end.

Aristotle proposed a formal vote of thanks to them all but especially to the children and the Peterson children in particular, 'without whose ability with the Stone,' he said, 'none of it could have happened. Your ancestor Alfred would be proud of you.'

'Now,' he went on, 'an extremely important announcement. At a worldwide M.I.C.E. teleconference yesterday evening I told the whole story including the courageous and determined part played by all four children. In recognition of this they were unanimously elected Honorary Council Members.'

There was cheering and an enthusiastic round of applause. The children did not really know what the elections meant but they knew it was a great honour and were pleased because it probably meant keeping in touch with everyone. So they stood up and said just that, along with a big thank you, to yet more applause.

At Aristotle's suggestion everyone stood up for a minute's silence in memory of the Colonel. Jess stood stiffly to attention as she had done many time before beside the Colonel at military parades.

Finally Liam presented Ian with a brand new pearl-handled catpin. 'Sorry, I didn't look after yours properly,' he said to much laughter.

There was a long and delicious lunch, at the end of which quite a lot of the animals were so full they just went to sleep.

'What a lot I shall have to tell Prudence and the babies,' said Dauntless Arvicola, thinking fondly of home. He had had some nut beer and the alcohol had taken his stammer away. His nose gave off a steady red glow.

When things had quietened down a little and it was nearly time to go, Aristotle came over to Olly and Tilly.

'About the Stone,' he said, 'what will you do with it?' Until that moment the children had assumed they would just hold on to it but when they came to think about it, they were not so sure.

'I think it should be kept here or at the M.I.C.E. Leeds place,' said Olly after a moment. 'Then if another threat arises, the Council can decide what to do. We don't have the contacts and sources of intelligence on our own.'

Tilly agreed. 'But if ever we have grandchildren,' she

added, 'we'll have to pass it on to them and let them decide what to do with it.'

'Wise decisions,' said Aristotle.

'I need hardly say,' he added, 'that you must keep the existence of M.I.C.E totally secret.' He told Daniel and Kiran the same thing.

'That'll be a challenge for you, Daniel,' said Kiran.

Olly and Tilly had a talk with Jess before they handed the Stone to Aristotle.

'The Colonel asked us to look after you but he really didn't need to.' said Tilly. 'We'd love you to come and live with us and Mum and Dad but also you could stay here in the village and live with Granny and Grandpa? You choose.'

Jess elected to stay. She had grown used to the village and liked Bill Peterson. She would be able to see the Akrams regularly, as well as Olly and Tilly when they came to visit. She would also be able to keep in touch with Section H.Q.

The grandparents were delighted. They were fond of Jess and upset about the Colonel's death. They were glad to help in carrying out his last wishes.

Later, when Olly and Tilly got Grandpa on his own, they told him the whole story. It was even more astounding than he had guessed. When they had finished he confessed that some weeks ago the Colonel had told him about being descended from Edwin and Odric and that there might be some trouble.

'I couldn't tell you, though,' he said, 'because he made me promise to keep it secret, but it was why I gave you the Stone.'

***

After that things got back to normal, except that two letters arrived for Olly and Tilly, several weeks apart.

The first was from a firm of lawyers in London:

Dear Sir and Madam,
Re: Colonel Edwin Scar-Foster deceased
We are the executors of the estate of the above and have
to inform you that in his Last Will and Testament he
devised and bequeathed to you jointly all his right title
and interest in fee simple in the property known as the
Antique Shop at Scar Bay together with the curtilage and
the contents thereof.
If you will kindly sign the enclosed papers we will make
arrangements to vest the aforesaid hereditaments in your
parents as trustees until you reach your majority.
Yours faithfully,
Bull, Wildgoose and Snipe,
Solicitors.

'Haven't a clue what it means,' they said to each other
but their father translated.

'The Colonel left a Will giving you the Antique Shop
in the event of his death.'

It caused a bit of a problem. Their parents knew it
was a valuable gift but they were so busy that they could
not see how to cope with it. They talked about it as
though it was a nuisance and the children thought they
would have to write back to say they could not accept,
until Granny came on the phone.

'Wonderful,' she said. 'Mrs Hutton and I have been
looking out for something like this. We'll run it for the
children until they're eighteen. Then they can decide for
themselves what to do with it. We'll have a lovely time.'

So that was settled.

The second letter was official-looking and came from
Buckingham Palace. It was easier to understand:

Dear Olly and Tilly,

Her Majesty the Queen has graciously decided to confer the Victoria Cross upon the late Colonel Edwin Scar-Foster, in recognition of his exceptional bravery and self-sacrifice in the service of the Crown.

It appears that he has no living relatives and Her Majesty has heard, from a reliable source, of your connection with him. She therefore believes it would be appropriate for you to attend Buckingham Palace to receive the medal on his behalf. Bearing in mind the fondness for dogs shared by Her Majesty and the late Colonel, she hopes that you will be able to bring Jess with you.

The letter gave a date when the ceremony would take place. The children wondered who the 'reliable source' was.

Their parents, of course, thought it was all to do with the Colonel rescuing them and his previously distinguished military service. They were pleased and knew it was something special but were overfaced with the difficulties.

'How will we get the dog there?' asked Mrs Peterson, looking harassed. 'We'll have to get it over from Scar Bay somehow then Dad and I will have to go with you to London and it's a weekday so we'll both have to take at least a day off work if not two and then there's the cost and so on.'

The grandparents came to the rescue.

'We'd love to take them to London and go to the Palace,' said Grandpa. 'It's a great honour for the family and anyway I need to be there to look after Jess. I know how busy you both are.'

The children silently cheered.

In the end it was a fantastic day. They travelled to London by train in a First Class coach specially reserved for them and others from West Yorkshire who were to receive medals and knighthoods for good works of various kinds. M.I.C.E. lent them the Stone so they could talk to Jess.

Ian and Liam got in touch with mice at the Palace and set up a secret video link so that everyone at Section H.Q. could watch the proceedings. Dauntless Arvicola and Aristotle made a special trip to the village on *S.S. Dauntless* and this time Prudence and the babies came. Kiran and Daniel (or Heli-Boy as she often now called him) were invited too.

At Buckingham Palace Olly, Tilly and Jess, with the others receiving honours, were treated with great respect by footmen.

When the name of the Colonel, together with those of the children and Jess, were called out they had to walk to the front of the gilded hall with everyone watching. Then a man in a scarlet and gold uniform read out a citation of the bravery of the Colonel and the Queen handed them the Colonel's medal in a velvet-lined box. She also pinned replicas on each of them, shook hands and stroked Jess's ears. At Section H.Q. everyone cheered and at the Palace everyone applauded. Olly bowed, Tilly attempted a curtsy and Jess wagged her tail enthusiastically.

Just as the applause was dying down and they were turning to go back to their seats, the Queen said quietly:

'Please give our kind regards to Mr Regdab.'

ABOUT THE AUTHOR

William Coniston lives in a small village in West Yorkshire, United Kingdom. He often shares a cheese soufflé with Ian, Liam and Jack.

You can read news about M.I.C.E. and some of the characters in this book on his Facebook author page and on Twitter.

Lightning Source UK Ltd.
Milton Keynes UK
UKHW042307260319
339964UK00001B/6/P